The Memory Hunter: Hunted by Secrets, Haunted by Truth

Timu Style

Published by Timu Style, 2024.

This is a work of fiction. Similarities to real people, places, or events are entirely coincidental.

THE MEMORY HUNTER: HUNTED BY SECRETS, HAUNTED BY TRUTH

First edition. November 17, 2024.

Copyright © 2024 Timu Style.

ISBN: 979-8230416418

Written by Timu Style.

Publisher Information

Copyright © 2024, **Timu Style**.
All rights reserved.
No part of this book may be reproduced, distributed, or transmitted in any form or by any means, including photocopying, recording, or other electronic or mechanical methods, without the prior written permission of the publisher, except in the case of brief quotations used for review purposes or academic references.

Under no circumstances will any blame or legal responsibility be held against the publisher, or author, for any damages, reparation, or monetary loss due to the information contained within this book, either directly or indirectly.

Before reading the book, please read the disclaimer.

For permissions, inquiries, or other correspondence:
timustyle@gmail.com

Disclaimer

The content of this book is a work of fiction. Names, characters, places, medical scenarios, and incidents are either the product of the author's imagination or are used fictitiously. Any resemblance to actual persons, living or dead, real-life medical events, organizations, or institutions is purely coincidental.

The medical procedures, treatments, and conditions described are for narrative purposes only and should not be interpreted as professional advice. Readers are advised not to use the medical information presented in this book as a substitute for consulting healthcare professionals or seeking proper medical care.

Neither the author, Timu Style, nor the publisher, **TimuStyle**, assumes any responsibility for actions taken based on the information contained within these novels. Any opinions expressed in the book are solely those of the author and do not represent the views of any affiliated institutions or organizations.

Chapter 1: The Memory Exchange

The office of the Memory Exchange buzzed with an eerie kind of silence, the kind filled with the hum of high-tech machinery and the occasional whirr of cooling fans. The walls were smooth, metallic silver, without a single blemish or hint of personalization. To some, the sterile environment was calming—a sanctuary of precision and order. To others, it was suffocating, a constant reminder of how deeply technology had infiltrated every corner of life. For Silas Kane, it was just another day at work.

He leaned back in his chair, letting his fingers drum against the polished steel desk. A holographic interface floated in the air in front of him, displaying rows of names, dates, and memory tags. He scanned the list with practiced ease, his mind already calculating the retrieval process for each entry. For Silas, memories weren't just snippets of the past; they were commodities, pieces of a person's identity that could be bought, sold, or, in his case, retrieved.

"Silas," a voice crackled through the comm system. It was Vera, his assistant and the only other person he trusted in this line of work. "Your ten o'clock is here."

Silas sighed, pushing himself upright. "Send them in."

The door slid open with a soft hiss, and a man stepped in, his face hidden beneath the shadow of a wide-brimmed hat. Silas recognized the type immediately—a nervous client. They were always the same: shifty eyes, clenched fists, the unmistakable air of someone about to confess a sin.

"Mr. Kane," the man said, his voice gravelly and low. "I hear you're the best."

"I am," Silas replied matter-of-factly, gesturing to the chair across from him. "Have a seat. Tell me what you need."

The man hesitated before sitting, his hands gripping the armrests as if they might anchor him in place. "I... I need you to retrieve a memory."

"That's what I do." Silas tapped a command into the interface, and a new screen materialized, ready to log the request. "But before we go further, you should know the rules. Memory retrieval isn't therapy, and it's not magic. If you're looking for closure or forgiveness, this isn't the place. All I do is find what's buried and bring it to the surface."

The man nodded, his jaw tightening. "I understand."

"Good. Now, whose memory are we talking about? Yours?"

The man shook his head. "No. It belongs to my brother. He disappeared six months ago, and the police... they've stopped looking. But I know there's something in his memories, something that can tell us what happened to him."

Silas raised an eyebrow. Third-party requests were always trickier, both legally and morally. "Do you have his consent on record?"

"I do," the man said quickly, pulling a data chip from his coat pocket and sliding it across the desk. "He signed it before he went missing. I uploaded it to the exchange's database, but no one will take the case. They say it's too risky."

Silas examined the chip before slotting it into the interface. The holographic screen flickered, displaying the consent form along with a photo of the missing man: Gideon Rourke, age 34. His face was sharp, angular, with piercing blue eyes that seemed to stare through the screen.

"I'll need to see his memory archive," Silas said. "Did he have a neural implant?"

"Yes. Standard model, linked to his private cloud. The credentials are on the chip."

Silas tapped another command, and a new interface appeared, accessing Gideon's memory cloud. Rows of memories organized by date and keyword populated the screen. Most of them were mundane—work meetings, family dinners, random snippets of daily life. But one sequence stood out, tagged with a red flag: **Restricted Access.**

"What's this?" Silas muttered, his fingers hovering over the flagged memories.

The man leaned forward, his eyes wide with urgency. "That's what I need you to retrieve. Those memories were locked before he disappeared. I think... I think someone didn't want him to remember."

Silas's gaze hardened. Tampering with someone's memories was a serious crime, and accessing restricted files came with its own set of risks. But curiosity had always been his weakness, and the promise of unraveling a mystery was too tempting to resist.

"I'll take the case," Silas said finally. "But this won't be cheap."

"Money isn't an issue," the man replied, sliding a second chip across the desk. "This should cover it."

Silas glanced at the chip's digital readout and whistled. The payment was generous, far more than he'd expected. "Alright," he said, pocketing the chip. "Let's get started."

The retrieval process was both art and science, a delicate balance of technical skill and psychological intuition. Silas began by syncing Gideon's neural data to his own equipment, creating a simulated environment where the memories could be reconstructed. The room darkened as the holographic interface expanded, filling the space with a web of glowing threads—Gideon's neural pathways visualized in intricate detail.

"Looks intact," Silas murmured, studying the threads. "No signs of corruption or decay. Whoever locked these memories knew what they were doing."

He tapped into the restricted section, bypassing the standard encryption protocols. As the lock dissolved, a flood of images and sensations rushed into the simulation: the smell of rain on asphalt, the sound of hurried footsteps, the flicker of neon lights in a dark alley. The memory began to take shape, coalescing into a vivid scene.

Silas felt the familiar pull as he immersed himself in the memory, his senses merging with Gideon's. He was no longer in his office but standing in the middle of a bustling city at night. The air was cold and damp, the streets slick with rain. Gideon was there, just a few feet ahead, his face tense with determination as he hurried through the crowd.

"What are you running from?" Silas whispered, following the phantom figure.

8

The memory shifted, the scene fracturing and reforming in flashes of color and sound. Gideon turned a corner, entering a dimly lit building. The walls were lined with old posters and graffiti, the air heavy with the scent of mildew. He climbed a narrow staircase, his footsteps echoing in the silence.

At the top of the stairs, a door loomed, its surface scarred with scratches and peeling paint. Gideon hesitated, his hand trembling as he reached for the handle. Then, with a deep breath, he pushed it open.

The room beyond was stark and empty, save for a single chair and a small table. On the table sat a device—a sleek, black cube humming with faint energy. Gideon approached it cautiously, his reflection distorted in its glossy surface.

"What is this?" Silas muttered, his pulse quickening.

As Gideon reached for the cube, the memory abruptly shattered, the fragments dissolving into static. Silas was yanked out of the simulation, his head spinning from the abrupt disconnection.

"Damn it," he growled, rubbing his temples. The retrieval had been cut off prematurely, leaving him with more questions than answers. But one thing was clear: whatever Gideon had found that night was the key to his disappearance.

Silas turned to the client, who had been watching the process with bated breath. "I've got part of the memory," he said. "But it's incomplete. I'll need more time to piece together the rest."

The man nodded, his expression a mix of hope and fear. "Do whatever it takes," he said. "Just find him."

Silas leaned back in his chair, his mind already racing with possibilities. This wasn't just another job; it was the beginning of something much bigger. And if he wasn't careful, it could also be the end of him.

Chapter 2: A Faded Thread

The sky outside Silas Kane's office was a washed-out gray, a fitting backdrop for the cold, synthetic hum of his workspace. The Memory Exchange, nestled in the heart of the city, was as much a symbol of progress as it was a monument to humanity's obsession with the past. In this world, memories were currency, and people like Silas were both brokers and scavengers of the mind.

Today, his client was late.

He leaned against the corner of his desk, his arms crossed as he glanced at the clock for the fifth time. Vera, his assistant, had buzzed him nearly twenty minutes ago to let him know the client was on their way. By now, they should have been in the chair across from him, spilling their secrets and handing over data chips like they were confessions.

Finally, the door slid open with a faint hiss. A woman stepped inside, her face obscured by the hood of her jacket. Her movements were cautious, deliberate, as though she were afraid the walls themselves might betray her.

"Ms. Laramie?" Silas asked, his tone even.

She nodded but didn't remove her hood. "I didn't know where else to go," she said softly, her voice trembling at the edges. "They told me you could help."

"They were right," Silas replied, gesturing to the chair. "Please, sit down."

She hesitated for a moment before taking the seat, her hands gripping the fabric of her jacket. Silas studied her face as she pulled back the hood. Her features were sharp but worn, the kind of face that carried the weight of too many sleepless nights. Her dark eyes darted around the room, as if searching for hidden threats.

"You're safe here," Silas said, his voice steady but not without empathy. "Why don't you start by telling me what you need?"

Ms. Laramie exhaled slowly, her gaze fixed on a point somewhere beyond the desk. "My sister," she began, her voice barely above a whisper. "She's missing. Has been for two years. The police filed it away as a cold case months ago, but... I know she didn't just disappear."

Silas leaned forward, his interest piqued. "Why come to me now?"

She hesitated, her hands clenching into fists. "Because I found this," she said, pulling a small, battered data chip from her pocket and sliding it across the desk.

Silas picked it up, turning it over in his hand. It was scratched and scuffed, its edges worn smooth from handling. "What's on it?"

"It's from her neural implant," Ms. Laramie said. "The last backup before she went missing. I thought... maybe there's something in her memories, something the police missed."

Silas frowned. Extracting memories from a missing person's implant was a legal gray area, even with a family member's consent. But he'd danced that line before, and something about Ms. Laramie's desperation made him reluctant to refuse.

"Alright," he said, slotting the chip into his interface. "Let's see what we're dealing with."

The holographic display flared to life, projecting rows of memory files in shimmering blue light. Most of the entries were ordinary, labeled with mundane tags like "Work," "Dinner," and "Phone Call." But as Silas scrolled through, he noticed a cluster of entries marked with a red flag, much like the restricted memories in Gideon Rourke's case.

"These flagged files," Silas said, gesturing to the display. "Do you know why they're restricted?"

Ms. Laramie shook her head. "No. She never told me about anything dangerous or secretive. But she... she was scared the last time I saw her. Like she knew something was coming."

Silas's jaw tightened. Fear wasn't something that just appeared in memories; it lingered, seeping into every detail like a watermark. Whatever her sister had experienced, it had left an indelible mark.

"I'll start with the flagged files," he said, his fingers already dancing across the interface. "But be warned: retrieval can be unpredictable. I might not get everything on the first pass."

"I understand," Ms. Laramie replied, her voice steady now. "Just... find her."

Silas slipped on the neural interface, a lightweight device that fit snugly over his temples. He activated the simulation, allowing the memory threads to weave around him in a complex web of light and sound. The world of the office faded away, replaced by the fragmented landscape of another person's mind.

The first memory emerged slowly, like a photograph coming into focus. Silas found himself in a small, dimly lit room. The walls were lined with bookshelves, their contents haphazardly arranged, and a faint smell of coffee lingered in the air. A woman—presumably Ms. Laramie's sister—sat at a desk, her back to him. Her shoulders were tense, her hands trembling as she typed on a sleek black keyboard.

"What are you working on?" Silas muttered, knowing full well she couldn't hear him.

The memory shifted, the scene rippling like a disturbed pond. The woman turned, her face pale and drawn. She was holding a small, metallic device—something that looked like a portable drive or a data chip.

"I shouldn't have taken it," she whispered, her voice barely audible over the hum of the memory. "But they were lying. I couldn't let them bury the truth."

Silas's pulse quickened. "What truth?"

Before he could gather more, the memory fractured, dissolving into static. He cursed under his breath as the simulation recalibrated, pulling him into the next flagged file.

The second memory was darker, both literally and figuratively. Silas stood in the middle of an empty parking garage, the air heavy with the smell of oil and concrete. Ms. Laramie's sister was there, pacing nervously as she clutched the same metallic device from before. Her breath came in short, panicked bursts, her eyes darting to the shadows.

A figure emerged from the darkness—a man in a dark coat, his face obscured by the brim of a hat. He approached slowly, his movements deliberate and menacing.

"You shouldn't have taken it," the man said, his voice cold and sharp. "You have no idea what you've done."

The woman backed away, clutching the device to her chest. "I did what was right. People deserve to know."

"They deserve to live," the man countered, his tone growing more threatening. "And if you don't hand it over, neither of us will."

The scene froze, the memory stuttering as if caught in a loop. Silas felt a sharp jolt in his head, a sign that the retrieval was hitting a firewall. He yanked himself out of the simulation, pulling off the neural interface with a groan.

Back in the real world, Ms. Laramie was staring at him, her hands gripping the edge of the desk. "Did you find anything?" she asked, her voice tight with anticipation.

"Fragments," Silas admitted, rubbing his temples. "But enough to know your sister was in trouble. She mentioned something about exposing the truth, and there was a man—someone who seemed very intent on stopping her."

Ms. Laramie's eyes widened. "Do you think he... he killed her?"

Silas hesitated. He'd seen enough in this line of work to know better than to jump to conclusions. "I don't know yet. But there's more to this than I expected. I'll need to run another session to piece together the rest."

Ms. Laramie nodded, her expression a mix of fear and determination. "Whatever it takes. I need to know what happened to her."

Silas leaned back in his chair, his mind already racing with possibilities. The memories he'd retrieved were just the beginning, a faded thread leading to something much larger.

But as he stared at the holographic display, he couldn't shake the feeling that pulling on that thread might unravel more than just the truth—it might unravel him as well.

Chapter 3: Fragments of the Past

The office lights dimmed as Silas prepared for another session, the faint hum of the memory retrieval equipment filling the silence. The memories of Ms. Laramie's sister, distorted and incomplete, lingered in his mind like a bad dream. He couldn't shake the image of her clutching the metallic device or the ominous figure threatening her in the shadows. It wasn't just a cold case anymore—it was a puzzle, and Silas had never been one to walk away from an unfinished puzzle.

He adjusted the neural interface on his temples, the device cool against his skin. The holographic display sprang to life once more, the rows of flagged files glowing faintly as they awaited his command. This time, he was diving deeper, pushing the boundaries of what was safe.

"Vera," he called out, his voice steady despite the knot in his stomach.

The comm system crackled in response. "Yes, Silas?"

"If I'm not out in thirty minutes, pull me out manually."

"Understood," she replied, her tone clipped but concerned. Vera had been through enough of Silas's high-risk retrievals to know when things could go sideways.

He exhaled, his fingers hovering over the interface. "Alright," he muttered. "Let's see where this rabbit hole leads."

With a flick of his wrist, he activated the next memory file.

The transition was seamless, the real world dissolving into a scene that felt both vivid and surreal. Silas found himself standing in the middle of a large, sterile laboratory. The air was thick with the acrid smell of chemicals, and the hum of machinery resonated in the background. Shelves lined the walls, filled with vials of liquid and stacks of data drives.

Ms. Laramie's sister was there, her face a mask of determination as she scanned a series of documents spread out on a metallic table. The metallic device from the previous memory sat next to her, its sleek black surface gleaming under the harsh fluorescent lights.

Silas moved closer, careful not to disturb the memory's fragile framework. He had learned long ago that memories were like cobwebs—delicate and easily torn apart if mishandled.

"What are you looking at?" he murmured, knowing she couldn't hear him but speaking out of habit.

As if in response, the memory shifted. The papers on the table blurred, their text smudging and reforming until a single word stood out: **"Aegis."**

Silas frowned. "Aegis?" The name tickled something in the back of his mind, a faint echo he couldn't quite place.

The memory rippled again, pulling him to another part of the room. This time, Ms. Laramie's sister was speaking in hushed tones to a man in a white lab coat. His face was partially obscured, but his voice carried a sense of urgency.

"You don't understand what you've done," the man said, his tone sharp. "If this gets out, they'll kill us both."

"Then let them," she shot back. "People deserve to know the truth."

The man shook his head, his expression a mixture of fear and frustration. "It's not just about the truth. It's about what they'll do to silence it. Aegis doesn't play games—they don't leave loose ends."

The memory fractured again, the scene dissolving into static. Silas felt a sharp jolt in his chest, like a phantom pain that wasn't his own. He clenched his fists, willing himself to stay grounded as the simulation recalibrated.

The next memory was darker, more chaotic. Silas found himself in a dimly lit alley, the ground slick with rain. Ms. Laramie's sister was running, her breath ragged as she clutched the metallic device to her chest. Behind her, shadows moved—figures in black suits, their faces obscured by masks.

"Stop!" one of them shouted, their voice muffled but commanding.

She didn't stop. She rounded a corner, her feet slipping on the wet pavement, and ducked into an abandoned building. Silas followed, his heart pounding in time with hers as the memory's tension gripped him.

Inside, the air was damp and stale, the faint smell of mildew clinging to the walls. She climbed a set of rickety stairs, each step creaking under her weight. At the top, she turned into a small room and locked the door behind her.

The figures outside weren't far behind. Silas could hear their muffled voices as they searched the building, their footsteps echoing through the halls.

In the room, Ms. Laramie's sister pulled a small recorder from her pocket. She pressed a button, her voice shaking as she spoke into it.

"If you're hearing this, it means I didn't make it. My name is Eleanor Laramie, and I've uncovered something that Aegis doesn't want you to know. They've been conducting experiments—dangerous ones—and they've been covering it up for years. The device I have contains the proof. Please, whoever finds this, don't let them get away with it."

The sound of splintering wood jolted Silas. The figures had found her. The memory froze, the scene flickering as if caught between frames.

"Damn it," Silas muttered, reaching out as if he could physically hold the memory together. The edges of the scene blurred, the details slipping through his fingers like sand. Before he could stabilize it, the memory collapsed entirely, leaving him in darkness.

When Silas came to, he was back in his office, his head pounding like a drum. He ripped off the neural interface, his breathing shallow as he tried to shake the disorientation.

"Silas!" Vera's voice crackled through the comm system. "Are you alright? You were in there for nearly forty minutes."

"I'm fine," he said, though the tremor in his voice suggested otherwise. "But this case... it's bigger than I thought."

He glanced at the holographic display, the word **"Aegis"** still etched into his mind. The name carried weight, though he couldn't quite remember why. It felt like an echo of something he had tried to forget.

Vera's voice softened. "You found something, didn't you?"

"I found pieces," Silas admitted. "Fragments of the past. But it's not just about Eleanor or her sister anymore. This... this is something else entirely."

He leaned back in his chair, his gaze fixed on the flickering display. As much as he wanted to focus on the case, his mind kept circling back to the jolt he had felt during the retrieval. It wasn't just a side effect of the simulation—it was something deeper, something personal.

For the first time in years, Silas felt the faint stirrings of his own suppressed memories, the shadows of a trauma he had buried long ago. And though he didn't want to admit it, he knew that unraveling Eleanor's mystery might mean facing his own.

Chapter 4: The Red String

The rain fell in relentless sheets outside the Memory Exchange, painting the glass windows with streaks of water that distorted the view of the city beyond. Silas Kane sat in his chair, elbows on his desk, staring at the holographic display before him. The word **"Aegis"** hovered like an accusation in the air, its glowing letters stark against the dim light of the office.

Silas reached for his coffee mug, only to find it empty. He sighed and pushed it aside, his mind churning over the fragments of Eleanor Laramie's memories. She had been running from something—or someone—and it was clear that the organization called Aegis was at the center of it all. But who were they? And why did the name feel so familiar?

"Vera," Silas called, breaking the silence.

Her voice crackled through the comm system. "What's up?"

"Pull up everything you can find on Aegis. Public records, news archives, anything."

Vera hesitated, and Silas could almost hear her skepticism through the line. "You know Aegis isn't exactly a public-facing entity, right? If they're involved in something shady, their tracks will be buried deep."

"I know," Silas replied, his tone sharp. "Just do what you can."

"Got it," Vera said, her voice softer now. "Give me a few minutes."

Silas leaned back in his chair, his fingers tapping a restless rhythm on the desk. He hated waiting, but this wasn't the kind of thing he could rush. Aegis was a thread, and if he pulled hard enough, it might unravel something far bigger than he was ready to face.

Minutes later, Vera's voice came back through the comm system. "You're not going to like this."

"Try me," Silas said, sitting up straight.

"I found a few mentions of Aegis in old government contracts," Vera began. "Mostly under the guise of research and development for advanced medical technologies. But here's the kicker: they're not listed as a standalone company. They're a subsidiary."

"Of who?"

"Omnicron Corporation," Vera replied, her tone heavy with implication.

Silas felt a chill run down his spine. Omnicron was a name everyone knew, a multinational conglomerate with fingers in everything from pharmaceuticals to artificial intelligence. They were the kind of entity that didn't just hold power—they defined it.

"Omnicron," Silas repeated, the word bitter on his tongue. "Of course it's them."

"It gets worse," Vera continued. "There's a pattern in the data. Every time someone files a lawsuit or whistleblower complaint against Omnicron, it gets swept under the rug.

Settlements, gag orders, missing plaintiffs—it's all there if you know where to look."

Silas's jaw tightened. "And Aegis?"

"No direct mentions," Vera admitted. "But if they're a part of Omnicron, it wouldn't be hard for them to hide in the shadows."

Silas stared at the holographic display, his mind racing. Eleanor Laramie had been onto something, and it had cost her everything. Now her sister had dragged him into the same web, and he wasn't sure he could find a way out.

"Thanks, Vera," he said finally. "Keep digging. I'll let you know if I need more."

"You always need more," Vera quipped, her tone light but her concern evident. "Be careful, Silas."

Silas turned his attention back to the fragments of Eleanor's memories. The recorder she had used, the mysterious device she had risked everything to protect—it all pointed to something Omnicron and Aegis didn't want the world to see. But he needed more than memories to connect the dots. He needed leads, tangible threads he could follow.

He pulled up the last known location of Eleanor's neural implant, a data point buried in the metadata of her memories. It led him to a part of the city he hadn't visited in years: The Fringe.

The Fringe was a sprawling network of abandoned warehouses and factories, a relic of the city's industrial past. It had become a haven for those who lived outside the system—hackers, smugglers, and anyone else who didn't want to be found. If Eleanor had been hiding there, it was for good reason.

Silas grabbed his coat and neural interface, slipping them into a worn leather bag. The rain hadn't let up, but he didn't care. He had a feeling that if he didn't act now, he might lose the trail forever.

The Fringe was as desolate as Silas remembered. The rain turned the cracked pavement into a mosaic of puddles, reflecting the dim glow of neon signs that flickered sporadically. He kept his head down, his hood pulled tight against the cold, as he navigated the labyrinthine streets.

He arrived at the address tied to Eleanor's implant, an old factory with boarded-up windows and rusted metal doors. The air smelled of decay and damp earth, a stark contrast to the sleek, sterile environment of the Memory Exchange.

Silas approached the door cautiously, his hand resting on the pulse scanner he kept hidden in his jacket. He pressed it against the lock, the device emitting a faint beep as it bypassed the outdated security system. The door creaked open, revealing a dark interior lit only by the faint glow of a single overhead light.

The room was empty save for a desk in the center, its surface cluttered with papers, wires, and a small black device that looked eerily familiar. Silas stepped closer, his pulse quickening as he recognized the sleek, metallic object from Eleanor's memories.

"This is it," he muttered, reaching out to examine it.

The moment his fingers touched the device, a sharp pain shot through his temples. He staggered back, clutching his head as flashes of light and sound filled his vision. Images he couldn't place—shattered glass, blood-streaked walls, the sound of a woman screaming—flooded his mind, blurring the line between past and present.

He dropped to his knees, gasping for breath as the pain subsided. The flashes faded, leaving him with a single, haunting thought: These weren't just Eleanor's memories. They were his.

When Silas finally regained his composure, he forced himself to focus on the device. It was lightweight, its surface smooth and unmarked. He turned it over in his hands, searching for any clues about its purpose. On the underside, he found a small engraving: **"Prototype 17-A"** followed by the Aegis logo.

His stomach churned. This wasn't just a piece of hardware—it was evidence, something that tied Aegis to whatever experiments Eleanor had uncovered. And now it was in his hands.

A sudden noise behind him made him freeze. He spun around, his pulse scanner raised, as a figure emerged from the shadows. It was a man in a black suit, his face obscured by a mask.

"You shouldn't be here," the man said, his voice cold and mechanical.

Silas didn't wait for a second warning. He ducked as the man lunged, narrowly avoiding the blade that sliced through the air where his head had been. He rolled to the side, his pulse scanner emitting a high-pitched whine as it charged.

The man lunged again, but this time Silas was ready. He fired the scanner, the pulse hitting the man square in the chest. The force sent him staggering back, but it wasn't enough to take him down.

Silas cursed under his breath, his mind racing as he searched for an exit. The door was blocked, and the only other way out was a narrow window high on the wall. He bolted for it, grabbing the desk to pull himself up.

The man recovered quickly, his footsteps closing in as Silas smashed the window with his elbow. Shards of glass rained down as he climbed through, the edges cutting into his hands and arms. He hit the ground outside, his knees buckling under the impact, but he didn't stop.

He ran, the rain soaking through his clothes as he disappeared into the maze of streets. Behind him, the man's voice echoed through the darkness: "You can't hide forever, Kane."

By the time Silas made it back to the Memory Exchange, his hands were trembling, and his head throbbed with a dull ache. He dropped the black device onto his desk, his bloodied hands leaving smudges on its surface.

Vera's voice came through the comm system, sharp with concern. "Silas, what the hell happened? You're a mess."

"I found something," he said, his voice hoarse. "Something big."

She didn't press for details, but her tone softened. "You need to rest. Whatever this is, it can wait."

Silas shook his head, even though she couldn't see him. "No, it can't. They know I'm involved now. If I don't figure this out soon, I might not get another chance."

He stared at the device, its smooth surface gleaming under the light. Aegis was the red string, and now that he'd started pulling, there was no turning back.

Chapter 5: Memory Bleed

Silas Kane wasn't a stranger to the dark side of memory retrieval. He had seen clients spiral into paranoia, lose themselves in fragments of their past, or worse, question what was real and what was reconstructed. He had always prided himself on his ability to stay detached, to approach each case as a professional without letting the echoes of other people's lives burrow too deeply.

But that wall of detachment was beginning to crack.

The office was eerily quiet as Silas sat at his desk, staring at the sleek black device he had retrieved from The Fringe. The blood from his earlier scuffle had dried on his hands, leaving faint smudges on his skin. He had cleaned the cuts but hadn't bothered to bandage them. His mind was too preoccupied, spinning in endless loops around Eleanor's memories, the Aegis logo, and the sudden, searing flashes of pain that had left him gasping on the factory floor.

Those flashes hadn't just been memories—they had felt real. Too real. And they weren't Eleanor's. They were his.

"Silas," Vera's voice crackled through the comm system, startling him.

He blinked, realizing he had been sitting in the same position for almost an hour. His coffee had gone cold, and the holographic display in front of him had dimmed into standby mode.

"What is it?" he asked, his voice rough.

"You look like hell," Vera said, her concern cutting through the static. "Whatever you're working on, take a break. You've been running on fumes since you got back."

"I don't have time for a break," Silas muttered, rubbing his temples. "Not when Aegis is involved."

There was a pause on the other end of the line. "Silas, you're bleeding."

He frowned, glancing down at his hands. The cuts weren't deep, but Vera was right—fresh blood had started to seep from one of them, trickling down his wrist.

"It's nothing," he said, reaching for a tissue to wipe it away.

"You need rest," Vera insisted. "You're pushing yourself too hard, and you know what happens when you overdo it with the neural interface."

Silas didn't respond. He knew exactly what happened: neural degradation, cognitive dissonance, and worst of all, **memory bleed.** It was a rare but dangerous side effect of repeated memory dives—when fragments of retrieved memories began to leak into the retriever's own mind, blurring the line between self and subject.

"It's under control," he lied, leaning forward to reactivate the display. "I just need to finish this."

Vera sighed but didn't argue. "Fine. But don't say I didn't warn you."

Silas synced the black device to his system, watching as the interface lit up with encrypted files. The device hummed faintly, its internal mechanisms working to resist his attempts at access. He leaned in, his fingers flying across the holographic keyboard as he bypassed the security protocols.

The first file unlocked with a soft chime, revealing a fragmented memory thread. Silas hesitated for only a moment before activating the neural interface. The device clamped onto his temples, and the world around him dissolved into the swirling, disjointed landscape of the retrieved memory.

He was in a room—a cold, sterile laboratory much like the one in Eleanor's earlier memories. But this time, the perspective was different. He wasn't an observer. He was **inside** the memory, experiencing it firsthand.

A man in a lab coat stood before him, his face sharp and angular, with piercing blue eyes that seemed to look right through Silas. The man was speaking, his voice calm but urgent.

"The prototype isn't ready," he said. "If we release it now, the consequences could be catastrophic."

Another figure entered the room, a woman with a commanding presence. She wore a sleek black suit, her movements precise and deliberate. "The board doesn't care about consequences," she said. "They care about results. Aegis exists to deliver results."

The memory shifted, the edges blurring as if the scene itself were resisting Silas's intrusion. He stumbled, gripping the edges of the desk in the memory as the perspective changed again.

Now he was in a darkened room, his hands trembling as he held the black device—the same one now sitting on his desk in the real world. He could feel its weight, its cold surface pressing against his palms. Voices echoed around him, distorted and distant.

"This isn't what we agreed to," he heard himself say, though the words felt foreign in his mouth. "This isn't what I signed up for."

The memory fractured, the pieces splintering like glass. Silas gasped as the scene dissolved into static, his neural interface struggling to process the corrupted data.

He ripped off the interface, his breath coming in ragged gasps. The office swam back into focus, but the disorientation lingered. His head throbbed, and his hands trembled as he reached for the coffee cup, only to knock it over.

"Damn it," he muttered, pushing himself away from the desk. His reflection in the darkened window caught his eye, and for a moment, he didn't recognize the man staring back at him.

"Silas," Vera's voice came through the comm system again. "I've been monitoring your vitals. Your heart rate spiked, and your neural activity is off the charts. What happened?"

"I'm fine," he said, though the words felt hollow.

"You're not fine," Vera shot back. "Your system flagged a potential memory bleed. You need to stop—now."

Silas clenched his fists, the tremors in his hands refusing to subside. He had heard about memory bleed cases, where retrievers began to lose their sense of self, their own memories overwritten by fragments of their clients'. It was a fate worse than death for someone in his line of work.

"I can handle it," he insisted, though doubt gnawed at the edges of his resolve. "I'm close to something big, Vera. I can't stop now."

Vera's voice softened. "You won't solve anything if you lose yourself in the process."

The hours blurred as Silas continued to sift through the files on the black device, each one revealing more pieces of the puzzle but leaving him with just as many questions. The name **Aegis** appeared again and again, tied to experiments labeled only as "Project Umbra."

One file caught his attention—a video recording buried deep within the device's encrypted archives. He hesitated, his finger hovering over the play button, before finally activating it.

The screen flickered to life, showing a man strapped to a chair in a dimly lit room. His face was pale, his eyes wide with fear. A voice offscreen spoke, calm and clinical.

"Subject 17-A, neural synchronization test. Begin extraction."

The man screamed as a helmet-like device was lowered onto his head, its metal prongs digging into his scalp. Silas flinched as the man's memories began to project onto the screen, chaotic images flashing by in rapid succession.

It was too much. Silas shut off the recording, his stomach churning. Whatever Aegis had been doing, it wasn't research—it was torture.

The next time Silas closed his eyes, he found himself back in the darkened room from the memory, holding the black device. The voices were louder now, accusing and relentless.

"You knew," one of them said. "You knew what they were doing, and you did nothing."

"I didn't—" Silas tried to protest, but the words stuck in his throat. The memory began to twist, the walls of the room closing in around him. He could feel the weight of the device in his hands, its cold surface burning against his skin.

"Stop!" he shouted, his voice echoing in the emptiness.

He woke with a start, his heart pounding as he realized he had fallen asleep at his desk. The office was dark, the only light coming from the faint glow of the holographic display. He rubbed his eyes, trying to shake the lingering images from his mind.

The line between memory and reality was beginning to blur, and Silas knew he was running out of time. If he didn't solve this case soon, he might not just lose his career—he might lose himself entirely.

The black device sat in the center of the desk, its sleek surface gleaming like a taunt. Silas stared at it, his mind a whirlwind of conflicting thoughts. He had spent years diving into other people's memories, unraveling their secrets and solving their mysteries. But now, for the first time, he felt like a part of the puzzle, a piece that didn't quite fit but couldn't be ignored.

He reached for the neural interface again, his fingers trembling as he prepared for another dive. The dangers didn't matter anymore. The answers were out there, buried in the fragments of the past, and Silas wasn't going to stop until he found them.

Chapter 6: Forgotten Faces

The morning light seeped through the blinds of Silas Kane's office, painting streaks of pale gold across the sleek surfaces of his workspace. He hadn't slept. The fragments of memories he'd extracted were circling in his mind like vultures over a carcass, relentless and haunting. The black device sat in the middle of his desk, its smooth, unassuming surface hiding secrets that were tearing at the edges of his sanity.

He leaned forward, his hands trembling slightly as he adjusted the neural interface on his temples. He told himself this dive would be the last, the one that would give him the breakthrough he needed to piece everything together. But a whisper of doubt lingered in his mind. What if the answers weren't out there? What if they were buried somewhere inside him?

"Silas," Vera's voice crackled through the comm system, jolting him.

"What is it?" he snapped, his nerves frayed.

"You need to stop," she said, her tone laced with concern. "You've been diving nonstop, and your vitals are all over the place. If you keep pushing like this—"

"I don't have a choice," Silas interrupted, his voice sharp. "I'm close to something. Something big."

Vera sighed, her frustration evident. "At least let me monitor you during the dive. If anything goes wrong—"

"I'll pull myself out," Silas said, though they both knew the promise was hollow.

Without waiting for her response, he activated the memory sequence.

The transition was jarring. One moment, Silas was sitting in his office; the next, he was standing in the middle of a bustling street. The air was thick with the scent of rain and asphalt, the sounds of the city blending into a chaotic symphony. He glanced around, his eyes catching on the signs and storefronts that lined the street. It was familiar—too familiar.

He knew this place.

It wasn't part of Eleanor Laramie's memories. It was part of his.

"What the hell?" Silas muttered, his pulse quickening.

The scene shifted, the colors bleeding together like a watercolor painting left in the rain. He found himself in a small apartment, the walls covered in faded wallpaper and the floor littered with books and papers. A woman stood in the kitchen, her back to him as she stirred a pot on the stove.

Silas froze, his breath catching in his throat. He knew her.

"Mom?" he whispered, his voice barely audible.

She turned, and for a moment, Silas felt like a child again, standing in the shadow of a figure who had once been his entire world. Her face was worn but kind, her eyes a soft brown that glimmered with warmth.

"You're late," she said, her tone light but teasing. "Dinner's almost ready."

Silas opened his mouth to respond, but the words wouldn't come. This wasn't real. It couldn't be real.

The scene shifted again, pulling him into another memory. This time, he was in a hospital room. The sterile smell of antiseptic filled the air, and the steady beep of a heart monitor echoed in the background. His mother lay on the bed, her face pale and drawn. A younger version of Silas sat in a chair beside her, his hands clenched into fists.

"Promise me," she said, her voice weak but steady. "Promise me you won't let them win."

"I don't understand," the younger Silas said, his voice trembling. "Who's them?"

She reached out, her hand resting lightly on his. "You will. One day."

The memory fractured, the edges dissolving into static as Silas gasped for air. He ripped off the neural interface, his head pounding as he tried to make sense of what he had seen.

Back in his office, Silas leaned back in his chair, his mind reeling. The memories had felt so real, so vivid, but they didn't belong to Eleanor Laramie. They were his own.

He ran a hand through his hair, his fingers trembling as he reached for a glass of water. The word **Aegis** echoed in his mind, a thread connecting his mother's cryptic warning to the tangled web he was now unraveling.

"Silas," Vera's voice came through the comm system again. "Your vitals spiked during the dive. What happened?"

"I..." Silas hesitated, unsure of how to explain. "I saw her. My mother."

Vera was silent for a moment, the weight of his words sinking in. "Silas, that's not possible. The memories you're retrieving—they're not yours."

"I know that," Silas snapped, though his voice betrayed his doubt. "But these were different. They weren't just fragments. They were... mine."

"Memory bleed," Vera said softly, the term hanging heavy in the air.

Silas shook his head, his frustration boiling over. "It's not just that. There's a connection. My mother—she knew something about Aegis. She warned me about them."

"Silas," Vera said gently, "your mother's been gone for years. Whatever connection you think she had to this case, it's not—"

"It is!" Silas interrupted, slamming his hand on the desk. "She's part of this. I don't know how, but she is."

Determined to find answers, Silas pulled up the encrypted files from the black device, his focus narrowing on a set of coordinates buried deep within the metadata. The location was remote, a facility on the outskirts of the city that had been abandoned for years.

It was a long shot, but it was the only lead he had.

The facility was a relic of a bygone era, its walls covered in rust and graffiti. The air was thick with the smell of decay, and the faint sound of dripping water echoed through the empty halls. Silas moved cautiously, his pulse scanner in hand as he navigated the labyrinth of corridors.

He found the lab in the basement, its walls lined with shelves of old equipment and dusty files. In the center of the room stood a console, its screen flickering faintly as if it had been left on standby for years.

Silas approached the console, his fingers brushing against the keys as he activated the system. The screen came to life, displaying rows of data and a series of video logs.

The first log showed a man in a lab coat—Dr. Marcus Kane. Silas's breath caught in his throat as he realized he was looking at his father.

"This is Project Umbra, day 187," Dr. Kane said, his voice calm but tinged with urgency. "The neural synchronization tests are yielding promising results, but the risks are... significant. Aegis is pushing for human trials, but I'm not sure we're ready."

The video cut off abruptly, replaced by another log. This time, Silas's mother appeared on the screen, her expression grim.

"If you're watching this, it means they've found us," she said. "Aegis won't stop until they've silenced everyone who knows the truth. Silas, if you're out there, you need to finish what we started. Don't let them win."

The screen went dark, leaving Silas staring at his own reflection. His mind raced as the pieces of the puzzle began to fall into place. His parents hadn't just been scientists working for Aegis—they had been whistleblowers, fighting to expose the truth about the organization's experiments.

And now, it was up to him to finish what they had started.

The drive back to the city was a blur, the weight of the revelations pressing heavily on Silas's chest. The memories, the warnings, the black device—it all pointed to one undeniable truth: Aegis wasn't just another corrupt corporation. They were something far worse, and they would stop at nothing to protect their secrets.

38

As Silas parked outside the Memory Exchange, he glanced at his reflection in the rearview mirror. For the first time in years, he saw not just a memory retriever, but a man with a purpose.

The forgotten faces of his past were no longer shadows. They were the spark that would light the fire.

Chapter 7: The Shadow Syndicate

The city skyline was a mosaic of glowing windows and flickering neon signs as Silas Kane stared out the rain-streaked window of his apartment. His mind was a labyrinth of questions, each one more dangerous than the last. The revelations from the abandoned facility had shattered the fragile barrier he'd built between his work and his past. Aegis wasn't just a corporate boogeyman—they were a hydra, their influence stretching into places Silas had never dared to imagine.

And now, they were watching him.

His pulse scanner sat on the coffee table, its soft hum a comfort in the stillness of the room. He reached for it instinctively, the cool metal fitting perfectly in his hand. Vera's voice crackled through the comm link on his desk.

"You're not seriously thinking of going out again tonight," she said, her tone a mix of concern and exasperation. "You've been diving non-stop, and now you want to take on a syndicate? Alone?"

"I don't have a choice," Silas replied, his voice low but firm. "If I don't move now, they'll bury this before I can dig any deeper."

"You're not invincible, Silas," Vera shot back. "These people aren't just criminals—they're untouchable. They have resources, connections. Hell, they probably know you're listening right now."

Silas paused, her words striking a nerve. He knew she was right. Aegis wasn't operating alone. The kind of power they wielded required more than just money—it required influence, the kind that could silence investigations and make entire people disappear.

But the thought of stopping wasn't an option. Not now. Not when he was so close.

Silas's first stop was the Memory Exchange. He bypassed the main office and headed straight for the secure archives, a labyrinth of data storage units housing decades of recorded memories. His credentials granted him access, but the tension in his gut told him this was the kind of move that got people killed.

He plugged the black device into the terminal, its screen lighting up with rows of encrypted files. He'd already decrypted most of them, but one set remained locked—files marked with the Aegis logo and a single, ominous phrase: **Project Umbra – Syndicate Operations.**

"Come on," Silas muttered, his fingers flying across the holographic keyboard. The encryption was dense, a digital fortress designed to repel even the most skilled hackers. But Silas wasn't just any hacker—he was a memory retriever. And memories always left breadcrumbs.

After what felt like an eternity, the final layer of encryption fell away, revealing a network map that stretched across the screen. Lines of connection crisscrossed like a spider's web, linking names, organizations, and locations. At the center of it all was Aegis, its reach extending into law enforcement, the judiciary, and even the federal government.

"Jesus," Silas whispered, his stomach twisting.

The nodes on the map revealed a list of high-ranking officials, each one tagged with notes indicating their roles: Judge R. Caldwell – "Asset acquired." Detective L. Moreno – "Handler." Senator D. Pierce – "Funding secured."

It wasn't just corruption. It was systemic control.

Silas leaned closer, his eyes narrowing as he spotted a name that made his blood run cold: Eleanor Laramie – "Liability neutralized."

A cold fury settled in his chest. They hadn't just been covering their tracks—they had been eliminating anyone who posed a threat to their operations. Eleanor had died for this. And if he wasn't careful, he'd be next.

The next name on the map led Silas to a high-rise office building downtown. Officially, it was the headquarters of a consulting firm specializing in logistics and supply chain management. Unofficially, it was the nerve center for the Shadow Syndicate—a covert group operating under the umbrella of Aegis, orchestrating everything from memory tampering to political assassinations.

Silas arrived under the cover of night, the city's rain-slicked streets providing a fitting backdrop for his descent into the belly of the beast. The building's exterior was unremarkable, its sleek glass façade blending seamlessly with the surrounding skyscrapers. But Silas knew better. The blandness was a façade, a mask hiding the rot beneath.

He slipped inside, the pulse scanner in his hand scanning the area for security systems. The lobby was quiet, its marble floors gleaming under the dim glow of recessed lighting. A lone security guard sat behind the desk, his attention focused on a small monitor displaying a live feed of the building's entrances.

Silas moved quickly, his steps silent as he approached the elevator bank. He bypassed the main controls, using a signal jammer to disable the surveillance cameras before prying open the control panel. The hidden keypad beneath was a standard Aegis design—efficient but predictable. He entered the override code he'd extracted from the device earlier, and the elevator doors slid open with a soft chime.

Inside, the panel displayed a standard list of floors, but Silas knew the real target lay below. He entered another code, and the display shifted, revealing a single word: **SUBLEVEL 3.**

The elevator descended smoothly, the hum of its motors the only sound. Silas tightened his grip on the pulse scanner, his nerves thrumming with anticipation. When the doors opened, he stepped into a corridor that reeked of antiseptic and cold metal.

The sublevel was a stark contrast to the polished corporate veneer above. The walls were bare concrete, the lighting harsh and fluorescent. Silas moved cautiously, his eyes scanning for signs of movement. He passed rows of rooms, their glass windows revealing labs filled with monitors, equipment, and rows of vials containing substances he couldn't begin to identify.

At the end of the corridor was a room labeled **SYNDICATE OPERATIONS.** Silas approached the door, his pulse scanner emitting a soft beep as it disabled the lock.

Inside, the room was dominated by a massive screen displaying a real-time feed of the network map he'd seen earlier, its web of connections pulsating like a living organism.

He approached the terminal, his fingers brushing against the keys. The data was overwhelming—dossiers, financial records, surveillance footage. Each file painted a picture of a syndicate so deeply embedded in the system that uprooting it seemed impossible.

But one file stood out: **Operation Mindveil.**

Silas opened it, his stomach sinking as he read the contents. The operation was a large-scale initiative to weaponize memory technology, using extracted memories to manipulate, blackmail, and control key figures across the city. The disappearances weren't random—they were calculated moves to silence dissent and secure power.

Before Silas could dig deeper, a voice behind him froze him in place.

"You've seen too much."

He turned slowly, his pulse scanner raised. A man stood in the doorway, his face obscured by the shadows. His voice was calm, almost casual, but the underlying threat was unmistakable.

"You're good, Kane," the man continued, stepping into the light. His face was sharp, his eyes cold and calculating. "But you should have walked away when you had the chance."

"And let you keep doing this?" Silas shot back, his voice steady despite the fear coiling in his gut. "Not a chance."

The man smirked, his expression devoid of humor. "You think you're the first idealist to come through here? The first to think they can take us down? You're out of your depth."

Before Silas could respond, the man lunged, his movements swift and precise. Silas fired the pulse scanner, the burst of energy hitting the man square in the chest, but it barely slowed him down. They grappled, the room filling with the sound of their struggle as Silas fought to keep control of the device.

The man slammed Silas against the terminal, his hand closing around his throat. "You should have stayed in your little office," he hissed.

With a surge of adrenaline, Silas drove his knee into the man's stomach, forcing him to release his grip. He grabbed the pulse scanner and fired again, this time aiming for the man's head. The blast sent him sprawling to the floor, unconscious.

Silas didn't wait to see if he would wake up. He grabbed a data drive from the terminal, its light blinking as it copied the files. When the process was complete, he yanked it free and bolted for the elevator.

Back in his apartment, Silas stared at the drive in his hand. It was a ticking time bomb, a collection of evidence that could expose the syndicate but also paint a target on his back.

He plugged it into his terminal, the screen lighting up with the data he had retrieved. Names, faces, connections—it was all there. But as he scrolled through the files, one entry made him pause.

His name. **Silas Kane – Subject 21.**

The room seemed to tilt as the implications hit him. He wasn't just a retriever. He was part of the experiment.

The Shadow Syndicate hadn't just found him. They had created him.

Chapter 8: Echoes of Trauma

The rain outside was relentless, its rhythmic pounding against the window blending with the hum of Silas Kane's terminal. He sat in his dimly lit apartment, the data drive from the Shadow Syndicate's headquarters clutched tightly in his hand. Its contents had shifted the ground beneath him. Every file he had decrypted, every connection he had uncovered, pointed to one unshakable truth: he wasn't just an outsider poking into Aegis's secrets. He was one of their creations.

Silas Kane – Subject 21.

The words blazed in his mind like a neon sign, impossible to ignore. His life, the fragments of memories he had always assumed were his own, now felt like a carefully constructed illusion. The thought turned his stomach, but there was no time to dwell on it. He needed answers, and he knew where to find them.

Silas reached for the neural interface, his hands trembling slightly as he adjusted it onto his temples. The device felt heavier than usual, the weight of what he was about to uncover pressing down on him. He had spent his career diving into other people's minds, extracting their secrets and piecing together their truths. But this time, he was diving into his own past—a past he had spent years trying to forget.

"Silas," Vera's voice crackled through the comm system, cutting through the silence. "You've been off the grid since last night. Please tell me you're not doing what I think you're doing."

"I don't have a choice," Silas replied, his voice low but resolute. "I need to know what they did to me."

"Then let me monitor you," Vera said, her tone pleading. "If something goes wrong—"

"I'll pull myself out," Silas interrupted, the lie slipping easily from his lips. "I'll be fine."

Vera didn't respond, but the silence on the other end of the line was heavy with disapproval. Silas took a deep breath, his fingers hovering over the activation key. "Here goes nothing," he muttered, and initiated the dive.

The transition was jarring, more so than any retrieval session he had experienced before. Silas felt like he was falling, the world around him dissolving into a swirl of colors and sounds. When the sensation finally stopped, he found himself standing in a familiar place: the living room of his childhood home.

The room was exactly as he remembered it, down to the worn couch with its frayed edges and the stack of books on the coffee table. The air was thick with the smell of coffee and cinnamon, a scent that transported him back to lazy Sunday mornings with his parents.

"Silas, come help me with the table," his mother's voice called from the kitchen.

He turned, his heart clenching at the sight of her. She looked younger than he remembered, her face free of the lines and wear that had marked her in the later years of her life. She was setting plates on the dining table, her movements quick and efficient.

"Mom," Silas whispered, his voice trembling.

She didn't respond, her attention focused on her task. Of course, she couldn't hear him—this wasn't real. It was a memory, a fragment of his past brought to life by the neural interface.

Silas took a step closer, his chest tightening as he watched her. He wanted to say something, to reach out and touch her, but he knew it would be futile. Instead, he stood there, drinking in the sight of her, until the memory shifted.

He was in the hospital now, the fluorescent lights casting a harsh glare on the sterile walls. His mother lay in the bed, her face pale and drawn. A younger version of himself sat by her side, his hands clenched into fists.

"I'm sorry," his mother said, her voice barely above a whisper. "I tried to protect you, but they wouldn't let me."

Silas watched as his younger self leaned closer, confusion etched on his face. "What are you talking about, Mom? Who wouldn't let you?"

She reached out, her hand trembling as she rested it on his. "Aegis," she said, her voice breaking. "They wanted you... for their experiments."

The memory fractured, the edges dissolving into static as Silas gasped for air. The hospital room blurred and reformed, pulling him into another scene.

This time, he was in a lab. The walls were lined with monitors displaying neural activity, and the air buzzed with the hum of high-tech equipment. He was strapped to a chair, his wrists bound and a helmet-like device clamped onto his head.

A man in a lab coat stood before him, his face sharp and angular, with piercing blue eyes that sent a chill down Silas's spine. "Subject 21 is ready," the man said, his voice calm but cold.

Silas struggled against the restraints, panic rising in his chest. "What are you doing to me?" he shouted, his voice echoing in the sterile room.

The man didn't answer. He adjusted the controls on the monitor, and a sharp pain shot through Silas's head. He screamed, the sensation unlike anything he had ever experienced. It was as if his mind was being torn apart, piece by piece.

"Begin synchronization," the man said, his tone devoid of emotion.

The memory fractured again, and Silas was thrown into a whirlwind of images and sensations. He saw flashes of his mother arguing with someone in a dimly lit office, her voice raised in anger. He saw himself as a child, sitting in a sterile room surrounded by strangers in lab coats. And he saw the Aegis logo, its stark design burned into his mind.

When the chaos finally subsided, Silas found himself back in the hospital room. His mother was gone, replaced by a figure he didn't recognize. The man was tall and imposing, his face obscured by shadows.

"You were never supposed to remember," the man said, his voice cold and menacing. "We made sure of that."

Silas took a step back, his heart pounding. "Who are you?"

The man stepped into the light, revealing a face that sent a jolt of recognition through Silas. It was the same man from the lab, the one who had overseen his experiments.

"You know who I am," the man said, a cruel smile playing on his lips. "I'm the one who made you."

Silas ripped off the neural interface, his chest heaving as he gasped for air. He was back in his apartment, but the room felt unfamiliar, like a place he no longer belonged. His hands trembled as he reached for the glass of water on the table, spilling half of it as he brought it to his lips.

"Silas!" Vera's voice crackled through the comm system, her tone panicked. "What happened? Your vitals went haywire."

Silas didn't respond. He couldn't. The memories were too fresh, too raw. They had unlocked something inside him, something he had spent years burying.

"I was one of them," he whispered, his voice barely audible. "I was part of their experiments."

Vera was silent for a moment, the weight of his words sinking in. "Silas," she said softly, "you need to stop. Whatever they did to you, it's in the past. You can't change it."

"I can't stop," Silas said, his voice trembling. "They took everything from me. My childhood, my mother... my life. I have to make them pay."

He stared at the neural interface on the table, his resolve hardening. The past was a nightmare he couldn't escape, but it was also the key to the truth. And Silas Kane wasn't going to stop until he uncovered every last piece.

Chapter 9: A Whispered Warning

Silas Kane sat at his desk, the black device from the Shadow Syndicate lying like an ominous centerpiece between him and the chaos of his terminal. Data logs scrolled across the holographic display, each line more damning than the last. Project Umbra, Syndicate Operations, Subject 21—it all pointed to a truth that Silas couldn't ignore but was too dangerous to fully comprehend.

The rain outside drummed against the window, a steady, relentless rhythm that matched the pounding in his head. He hadn't slept since the last dive into his memories, and the weight of what he had uncovered lingered like a heavy fog over his mind.

Then came the ping.

At first, Silas thought it was another notification from Vera. But the sound was different—softer, almost hesitant. His terminal screen blinked, and a new message appeared, marked with no sender and encrypted with layers of code.

You're closer than you think. But stop digging before it's too late.

Silas frowned, his fingers hovering over the keyboard. He had seen his fair share of cryptic messages, but this one carried an urgency that set his nerves on edge.

He typed a reply: **Who are you?**

The response came almost instantly: **Someone who wants to see you live through this. Meet me at the corner of Varick and Pine. Midnight. Come alone.**

Silas stared at the screen, his mind racing. It could be a trap, a calculated move by Aegis or the Syndicate to silence him once and for all. But it could also be the lead he desperately needed.

He made his decision in seconds.

The streets of the city were deserted as Silas approached the corner of Varick and Pine. The rain had let up, leaving the pavement slick and reflective under the glow of streetlights. He kept his pulse scanner tucked inside his coat, his senses on high alert as he scanned the area for any signs of movement.

A figure emerged from the shadows, their face obscured by the hood of a raincoat. They stood beneath a flickering streetlight, their posture tense but not overtly threatening.

"You came," the figure said, their voice low and distorted. It was impossible to tell if it belonged to a man or a woman.

"Who are you?" Silas demanded, keeping his distance.

The figure raised a gloved hand, motioning for him to lower his voice. "Names don't matter. What matters is that you're playing a dangerous game."

Silas took a cautious step closer, his grip tightening on the pulse scanner hidden in his pocket. "If you've got something to say, say it. I don't have time for theatrics."

The figure chuckled softly, a sound devoid of humor. "You're bolder than I expected. But boldness won't save you from what's coming."

Silas's patience was wearing thin. "Enough with the riddles. Why did you contact me?"

The figure tilted their head, their hood casting a shadow over their face. "Because you're not like the others. You're not just a retriever, Silas. You're one of them."

Silas felt a chill run down his spine. "One of who?"

The figure stepped closer, their voice dropping to a whisper. "Subject 21. Aegis created you, just like they created me."

The revelation hit Silas like a punch to the gut. He had suspected as much, but hearing it confirmed was something else entirely.

"Why?" he asked, his voice barely audible. "Why would they do this?"

The figure hesitated, their gloved hands clenching into fists. "Because we were experiments. Tests for Project Umbra. They wanted to see if they could weaponize memory extraction, if they could turn people like us into tools for manipulation and control."

"And Eleanor?" Silas pressed. "What about her?"

The figure stiffened. "She got too close. She found out about the Syndicate, about their operations. She tried to expose them, but they silenced her—just like they've silenced everyone else who's dared to stand against them."

Silas's mind raced as he processed the information. Eleanor's death, his mother's warnings, the Shadow Syndicate—it was all connected. But there was still so much he didn't understand.

"Why are you helping me?" he asked, his suspicion creeping back into his voice. "If you're one of them, why not turn me in?"

The figure sighed, their shoulders slumping. "Because I got out. I escaped before they could finish what they started. But you... you're still in their sights. They're watching you, Silas, waiting for you to make a mistake. If you keep digging, you'll end up like Eleanor."

Silas clenched his fists, the weight of the warning settling heavily on his chest. "I can't stop," he said, his voice firm. "They've taken too much from me. I need to know the truth."

The figure nodded slowly, as if they had expected his answer. "Then you need to be smart about it. Aegis isn't just a corporation—they're a machine, and the Syndicate is their shadow. If you want to survive, you'll need to stay one step ahead."

They reached into their pocket and pulled out a small data chip, handing it to Silas. "This is everything I have on Project Umbra. It's not much, but it's a start."

Silas took the chip, his fingers brushing against the cold metal. "What about you? Why not fight with me?"

The figure laughed softly, a bitter sound. "Because I've already lost too much. I'm not a hero, Silas. I'm just a ghost."

Before Silas could respond, the figure turned and disappeared into the shadows, leaving him alone beneath the flickering streetlight.

Back in his apartment, Silas plugged the data chip into his terminal, the screen lighting up with a series of files. Most of them were incomplete, corrupted fragments of research notes and surveillance logs. But one file stood out: a video recording marked **"Subject 21 – Observation Log."**

Silas hesitated, his heart pounding as he hovered over the play button. He wasn't sure if he was ready for what he might see, but he knew he didn't have a choice.

The video began, its grainy footage showing a younger version of himself strapped to a chair in a sterile lab. A man in a lab coat stood beside him, his face partially obscured by the frame.

"Subject 21 shows remarkable resilience," the man said, his voice calm and clinical. "Neural synchronization is stable, and memory implantation tests have been successful. However, long-term effects remain unpredictable."

The younger Silas struggled against the restraints, his voice muffled as he shouted something inaudible. The man ignored him, continuing to adjust the controls on the monitor.

"Proceed with Phase Three," the man said, his tone cold. "Let's see how far we can push him."

The video cut off abruptly, leaving Silas staring at the blank screen. His hands were trembling, his breath coming in shallow gasps. The memories, the experiments, the warnings—it was all too much.

But he couldn't stop now.

Silas leaned back in his chair, his mind racing as he tried to piece everything together. The anonymous figure's warning was clear: if he kept pushing, he was putting himself in unimaginable danger. But walking away wasn't an option. Not when the stakes were this high.

He stared at the terminal, the fragments of data blinking back at him like a challenge. Aegis and the Syndicate thought they could control him, thought they could silence him.

They were wrong.

Silas Kane wasn't just another experiment. He was a reckoning, and he was just getting started.

Chapter 10: Unseen Connections

The room was silent except for the faint hum of Silas Kane's terminal, its holographic display casting an eerie glow across his cluttered desk. Files from the mysterious data chip blinked on the screen, fragments of logs, surveillance footage, and corrupted reports forming a maddeningly incomplete picture. Each piece hinted at something catastrophic, yet the full scope of the truth remained frustratingly out of reach.

Silas rubbed his temples, exhaustion pressing down on him like a lead weight. The anonymous figure's warning echoed in his mind—*"They're watching you, Silas. Waiting for you to make a mistake."*

Mistakes weren't an option now. The stakes were too high.

He focused on one file labeled **"Target Acquisition – Tier Alpha,"** the title alone setting off alarms in his head. A single keystroke brought up a list of names and dates, each accompanied by a short note:

- **Eleanor Laramie**: "Classified materials recovered. Status: Neutralized."
- **Dr. Marcus Kane**: "Project Umbra oversight. Status: Deceased."

- **Nadine Cross**: "Algorithm architect. Status: Missing."
- **Noah Vreeland**: "Phase Two subject. Status: Missing."

Silas's breath caught when he saw his own name at the bottom of the list:

- **Silas Kane**: "Phase Three subject. Status: Active."

His fingers trembled as he scrolled back up, his eyes locking onto Eleanor's entry. "Classified materials recovered." The cryptic note sent a chill down his spine. He had uncovered fragments of her memories, glimpses of the truth she had died for, but this file suggested she had known even more than he had realized.

The missing individuals weren't random victims of the Shadow Syndicate's experiments—they were key players, each tied to a devastating secret Aegis was desperate to keep buried.

Silas leaned back in his chair, letting the revelation settle over him. His father, Dr. Marcus Kane, wasn't just a scientist who had crossed paths with Aegis—he had been integral to Project Umbra's development. His mother's cryptic warnings, the experiments in Silas's own past, and the deaths of countless others all pointed to a single, horrifying conclusion: Aegis had been constructing something far bigger than memory manipulation.

But what was the endgame?

He needed more than fragmented files and ominous warnings. He needed someone who could help him make sense of the data.

Vera's voice broke through the haze of his thoughts, crackling over the comm system. "Silas, you've been quiet for hours. What's going on?"

"I'm connecting the dots," Silas replied, his voice heavy with exhaustion. "And it's worse than I thought."

"Define 'worse,'" Vera said, her tone edged with concern.

Silas hesitated, his eyes scanning the list of names on the screen. "The missing people—they weren't just test subjects. They were architects. They knew things, built things. Aegis didn't just take them; they erased them."

"Erased?" Vera echoed, the word hanging in the air like a guillotine.

"Eleanor was trying to expose something, and they killed her for it," Silas said, his voice hardening. "My father—he wasn't just part of the project. He was running it. And now they've turned me into one of their experiments."

Vera was silent for a long moment. When she finally spoke, her voice was quiet but steady. "What's the secret, Silas? What's so devastating that they'd kill to protect it?"

"I don't know," Silas admitted, his frustration boiling over. "But I'm going to find out."

The next file Silas opened was a heavily encrypted report marked **"Umbra – Phase Four Initiation."** It took him nearly an hour to crack the code, but when the contents finally appeared, they made his blood run cold.

The report detailed a plan to use memory extraction and implantation to control key figures in government, law enforcement, and corporate leadership. The missing individuals had been instrumental in developing the technology—a neural synchronization algorithm capable of rewriting a person's memories and, by extension, their identity.

The implications were staggering. With this technology, Aegis could create puppets out of anyone, molding their thoughts, actions, and loyalties to suit their needs. It wasn't just about control—it was about erasing free will.

Silas's stomach churned as he read the final paragraph:

"Phase Four requires the synchronization of a prototype subject. Subject 21 has shown promising results, with neural stability exceeding projected parameters. If successful, Subject 21 will serve as the keystone for full-scale implementation."

He slammed his fist against the desk, his frustration spilling over. He wasn't just a victim of Aegis's experiments—he was the linchpin in their plan.

Desperate for answers, Silas searched the files for anything that could tell him more about the missing individuals. One name stood out: **Nadine Cross.** The note beside her name—"Algorithm architect. Status: Missing"—suggested she had been instrumental in creating the technology Aegis was now weaponizing.

Silas pulled up her personnel file, hoping to find a lead. The file included a photo of a woman in her late thirties with sharp features and piercing green eyes. Her credentials were impressive: a PhD in computational neuroscience, multiple patents in neural interface design, and a tenure at a cutting-edge AI lab.

Her last known address was listed as an apartment in the city's tech district. It was a long shot, but it was all Silas had.

The tech district was a stark contrast to the rest of the city, its sleek, modern buildings bathed in the glow of holographic advertisements. Silas kept his head down as he navigated the crowded streets, his pulse scanner hidden beneath his coat.

When he reached Nadine's apartment building, he found the lobby deserted, its sterile white walls and minimalist décor giving it the feel of a high-end hospital. The security system was more advanced than he had anticipated, but Silas's skills—and his determination—were more than a match.

He bypassed the lock on her door, slipping inside with a sense of urgency. The apartment was eerily quiet, its sparse furnishings suggesting it hadn't been lived in for some time. Silas searched the space quickly but methodically, his eyes scanning for anything that might point to where Nadine had gone.

He found it in the form of a hidden compartment beneath her desk. Inside was a data drive, its casing marked with the Aegis logo.

Back in his apartment, Silas plugged the drive into his terminal, his heart racing as he accessed its contents. The files were a goldmine of information, detailing the inner workings of the neural synchronization algorithm and its potential applications.

But one file stood out—a video recording labeled **"To Whoever Finds This."**

Silas opened it, and Nadine's face appeared on the screen. She looked tired, her eyes heavy with a mixture of fear and determination.

"If you're watching this, it means they've found me," she began, her voice steady despite the gravity of her words. "My name is Nadine Cross, and I was part of Project Umbra. I helped build the algorithm they're using to control people. I thought it was going to revolutionize mental health treatment, but I was wrong."

She paused, her gaze intense. "Aegis is using the technology to rewrite memories, to turn people into puppets. They've already started with key figures—judges, senators, CEOs. They're building an empire of obedience, and they'll stop at nothing to complete it."

Nadine leaned closer to the camera, her expression urgent. "If you want to stop them, you'll need to find the original algorithm. It's hidden in a secure server farm outside the city, buried deep beneath layers of encryption. But be warned: they'll kill anyone who gets close."

The video ended abruptly, leaving Silas staring at the blank screen. The pieces were finally coming together, but the picture they formed was darker than he had ever imagined.

Aegis wasn't just manipulating memories. They were building a future where freedom was a relic of the past.

Silas leaned back in his chair, the weight of the revelations pressing down on him. The missing individuals weren't just victims—they were the architects of Aegis's dark vision, people who had been silenced because they knew too much.

And now, Silas was the only one left who could stop them.

The risks were higher than ever, but he knew one thing for certain: he wasn't going to back down.

Chapter 11: Hunted by Shadows

The night was thick with rain, a cold drizzle that slicked the city streets and reflected the neon signs of a sleepless world. Silas Kane moved like a shadow through the alleys, his hood pulled low over his face. He clutched the small data drive in his pocket—a ticking time bomb of truth. The revelations it contained about Project Umbra and Aegis's sinister plans could shatter lives, but the knowledge came with a price. He was no longer just a man with questions. He was a target.

The first sign that something was wrong had come an hour ago. As Silas decrypted more of the files from Nadine Cross's drive, his terminal had flashed with a security breach warning. Aegis's reach was long, and the moment he had accessed the sensitive data, they had locked onto him.

Now, they were hunting him.

Silas ducked into a narrow side street, his boots splashing in shallow puddles. He paused beneath a flickering streetlamp, scanning his surroundings. His pulse scanner buzzed faintly in his pocket, a subtle reminder that he wasn't alone.

A soft shuffle of footsteps echoed behind him.

Silas froze, every muscle in his body tensing. The rain muffled most sounds, but he had spent enough time in the underbelly of the city to recognize when someone was following him. Slowly, he reached into his coat, his fingers wrapping around the grip of the pulse scanner.

The footsteps grew louder, their rhythm deliberate and unhurried. Whoever was tailing him wasn't trying to hide.

Silas turned sharply, his pulse scanner raised. The alley was empty, the shadows playing tricks on his eyes. His breath came in shallow gasps as he backed away, his senses on high alert.

Then he saw it—a flicker of movement at the edge of his vision. A figure stepped into the dim light, their face obscured by a mask. They were dressed in black, their stance calm but predatory.

"Silas Kane," the figure said, their voice distorted by a modulator. "You've been busy."

Silas didn't answer. He fired the pulse scanner, the burst of energy lighting up the alley like a flash of lightning. The figure dodged with inhuman speed, their movements fluid and precise.

"You're making this harder than it needs to be," the figure said, their tone almost amused. "Hand over the drive, and we can end this quickly."

Silas's mind raced as he calculated his next move. He couldn't outrun them, not here. His only option was to fight.

The figure lunged, and Silas barely managed to sidestep the attack. He fired the pulse scanner again, the shot grazing the figure's shoulder. They staggered but didn't fall, their resilience confirming what Silas already suspected: this wasn't an ordinary pursuer. Aegis had sent one of their enforcers, a trained operative enhanced by the very technology they sought to protect.

Silas reached for a metal pipe leaning against the wall, wielding it like a makeshift weapon. The figure moved with precision, their strikes calculated and deadly. Silas parried as best he could, the clang of metal against metal echoing through the alley.

"You're outmatched," the figure said, their voice cold and detached. "You can't win."

Silas gritted his teeth, his determination outweighing his fear. "I don't need to win," he said. "I just need to survive."

With a burst of adrenaline, he swung the pipe in a wide arc, catching the figure off guard. They stumbled, and Silas seized the opportunity to fire the pulse scanner point-blank. The burst of energy sent the figure crashing into the wall, their body slumping to the ground.

Silas didn't wait to see if they would get up. He turned and ran, his lungs burning as he sprinted down the alley. The city blurred around him, a kaleidoscope of neon lights and rain-soaked streets. He needed to find a safe place to regroup, to figure out his next move.

He ducked into an abandoned warehouse on the outskirts of the tech district, the heavy metal door groaning as he pushed it shut behind him. The air inside was stale, the faint smell of rust and decay lingering in the shadows. Silas leaned against the wall, his chest heaving as he caught his breath.

The silence was oppressive, broken only by the occasional drip of water from the leaky roof. Silas pulled out the data drive, its faint glow a reminder of the danger he was in. He couldn't stop now—not when he was so close to exposing the truth.

A sudden noise snapped him out of his thoughts. Footsteps echoed through the warehouse, their sound amplified by the cavernous space. Silas's heart raced as he realized he wasn't alone.

He crouched behind a stack of rusted metal crates, his pulse scanner clutched tightly in his hand. The footsteps grew louder, more deliberate. Whoever was out there wasn't hiding—they were hunting.

Silas peeked around the edge of the crates, his eyes narrowing as he spotted three figures moving through the shadows. They were dressed in black, their faces hidden behind masks. Each one carried a weapon, their movements coordinated and efficient.

"Aegis doesn't mess around," Silas muttered under his breath.

The lead figure stopped, their head tilting as if they had heard him. "Fan out," they said, their voice sharp and commanding. "He's here."

Silas's mind raced as he weighed his options. He couldn't take on all three of them, not in a straight fight. His only chance was to outmaneuver them, to use the warehouse's layout to his advantage.

The next few minutes were a deadly game of cat and mouse. Silas moved silently through the maze of crates and machinery, his every step calculated to avoid detection. The enforcers searched methodically, their movements precise and unrelenting.

Silas reached the far end of the warehouse, where a rusted staircase led to an upper level. He climbed it quickly, the metal groaning under his weight. From the higher vantage point, he could see the enforcers below, their flashlights cutting through the darkness.

One of them stopped, their flashlight sweeping across the floor. They knelt, their fingers brushing against a wet footprint Silas had left behind.

"He went this way," they said, their voice cutting through the silence.

Silas cursed under his breath, his grip tightening on the pulse scanner. He needed to act fast. He scanned the upper level, his eyes landing on a large industrial hook suspended from a crane. An idea formed in his mind—dangerous, but it might just work.

Silas crept toward the control panel for the crane, his movements slow and deliberate. He powered it on, the hum of the machinery drawing the enforcers' attention.

"What was that?" one of them asked, their flashlight snapping toward the upper level.

Silas didn't hesitate. He activated the crane, the hook swinging wildly as it descended toward the enforcers. They scattered, their movements frantic as the hook crashed into a stack of crates, sending debris flying.

The distraction gave Silas the opening he needed. He fired his pulse scanner, the bursts of energy catching one of the enforcers in the chest. They fell with a grunt, their weapon clattering to the floor.

The remaining two enforcers regrouped, their weapons trained on the upper level. Silas ducked behind a support beam, his heart pounding as he calculated his next move.

"You're outnumbered, Kane," one of them called. "Surrender now, and we might let you live."

Silas smirked, despite the fear gnawing at the edges of his resolve. "You're going to have to do better than that."

The fight was brutal and chaotic, the confined space amplifying every sound. Silas moved with a combination of desperation and determination, using every tool at his disposal to keep the enforcers off balance.

By the time it was over, the warehouse was silent once more. Silas stood amidst the wreckage, his breath coming in ragged gasps. The enforcers lay unconscious around him, their weapons scattered across the floor.

He didn't stay to revel in his victory. He knew more would come—Aegis wouldn't stop until he was silenced. Clutching the data drive, Silas slipped out of the warehouse and into the night, his mind racing with the knowledge that the truth was closer than ever.

But so were the shadows that sought to consume him.

Chapter 12: False Memories

The night air was cold against Silas Kane's skin as he stumbled back into his apartment, every step weighted with exhaustion and dread. He locked the door behind him, the click of the deadbolt sounding louder than usual in the stillness. The room was a mess—papers scattered across his desk, a half-eaten sandwich sitting stale on the table—but Silas barely noticed. His mind was a storm of questions with no clear answers.

He dropped into his chair, pulling out the data drive he'd risked his life to protect. The truth about Aegis and their plans lay within, yet it felt like a curse more than a revelation. The events of the past few hours—the chase, the fight in the warehouse, the desperate need to stay one step ahead—had left him shaken. But what haunted him most was a seed of doubt that had taken root deep in his mind.

What if my memories aren't real?

The question had first surfaced during the dive into Nadine Cross's files. As Silas decrypted more of the data, he'd stumbled upon a report marked **"Subject Memory Recalibration – Case Study: S21."** His chest had tightened at the sight of the designation, knowing full well it referred to him. But what the report revealed had been far worse than he'd imagined.

The document described a series of memory implantation tests performed on him during his time as a subject in Project Umbra. The goal was to see if artificial memories could be seamlessly integrated into a person's consciousness, creating a false narrative that felt as real as the truth.

Silas had read the words over and over, his stomach churning as he processed their implications. The report claimed the tests were "largely successful," with only minor inconsistencies detected during neural synchronization scans. It had concluded with a chilling recommendation: *Proceed with full-scale memory recalibration.*

Now, seated at his desk with the city lights flickering beyond the window, Silas couldn't shake the feeling that his past was a carefully constructed lie. The memories he had relied on for so long—of his parents, his childhood, the life he thought he had lived—suddenly felt fragile, like a house of cards teetering on the edge of collapse.

He pulled up his terminal, the holographic interface springing to life. The files from the data drive were still there, waiting to be examined, but Silas hesitated. A part of him wanted to dig deeper, to uncover the full extent of Aegis's manipulations. But another part—the part driven by fear—was terrified of what he might find.

He rubbed his temples, trying to ground himself. *Think, Silas. What do you know for sure?* The question echoed in his mind, but the answer was elusive. Every memory, every moment, now carried a shadow of doubt.

The first memory he questioned was one he had clung to for years: the day his mother warned him about Aegis. He had been a teenager, sitting by her hospital bed as she struggled to explain the danger they were in. Her words had been cryptic, but they had stuck with him, shaping his path and fueling his determination to uncover the truth.

But what if that memory wasn't real? What if it had been planted, a carefully engineered fabrication designed to push him toward a specific goal? The idea made his stomach twist. If he couldn't trust his own memories, what could he trust?

He accessed the neural logs he had extracted during his previous dives, searching for anomalies. The interface displayed a web of interconnected nodes, each representing a fragment of his memories. As he navigated the network, he noticed something strange—certain nodes were darker than others, their edges frayed and unstable.

"What the hell is this?" Silas muttered, leaning closer to the screen.

He selected one of the unstable nodes, his heart racing as the memory unfolded before him.

He was back in his childhood home, the scent of cinnamon and coffee filling the air. His mother was in the kitchen, her movements fluid and graceful as she prepared breakfast. Silas sat at the table, a book open in front of him.

"Silas," his mother said, her voice warm and familiar. "You'll be late for school."

The memory felt vivid, real, but something was off. Silas couldn't put his finger on it at first, but as he focused, he realized the edges of the scene were blurry, like an old photograph starting to fade.

"What is this?" Silas muttered, his voice trembling.

The memory rippled, the scene shifting. Now he was standing in a hospital room, his mother lying in bed as she reached for his hand. Her voice was faint, her words barely audible.

"Aegis," she whispered. "They're dangerous. Promise me... promise you'll stop them."

Silas watched, his chest tightening as the memory fractured, the pieces swirling around him like shards of glass. He was pulled out of the dive, his neural interface disconnecting with a sharp jolt.

Back in the real world, Silas ripped off the neural interface, his breath coming in ragged gasps. His head throbbed, the edges of his vision tinged with static. He stared at the screen, the unstable nodes still pulsing faintly.

"They tampered with them," he said aloud, the realization hitting him like a freight train. "They've been rewriting my memories."

The implications were staggering. Every moment, every decision he had made, could have been influenced by Aegis's manipulations. The life he thought he had lived might be nothing more than a carefully constructed illusion.

The fear of losing himself, of being nothing more than a puppet controlled by Aegis, ignited a fire within Silas. He needed to know the truth, no matter how painful or dangerous it might be.

He accessed another node, this one labeled **"Primary Incident – Subject 21."** The memory unfolded slowly, its edges sharp and unyielding.

Silas was in a lab, the air thick with the hum of machinery. He was strapped to a chair, a helmet-like device clamped onto his head. The man standing before him was familiar—sharp features, piercing blue eyes—but his face was twisted with something Silas couldn't quite identify. Pity? Resignation? Or was it guilt?

"This will only hurt for a moment," the man said, his voice cold and detached.

Pain shot through Silas's head, a blinding white-hot sensation that made him scream. The memories flooded in, disjointed and chaotic—faces he didn't recognize, places he had never been, moments that weren't his.

"Phase Two complete," the man said, his tone clinical. "Proceed with Phase Three."

The memory shattered, pulling Silas back into the real world. He clutched his head, the pain lingering like an echo of the experiment.

Silas sat in silence, the weight of the truth pressing down on him. Aegis hadn't just tampered with his memories—they had built him. Every thought, every emotion, every decision he had ever made was tainted by their influence.

But they had underestimated him.

Silas wasn't just a subject. He was a survivor. And he wasn't going to let Aegis win.

He stared at the data drive on his desk, his resolve hardening. The answers he sought were buried deep, but he would find them. He had to. Because the truth wasn't just about him—it was about everyone Aegis had silenced, manipulated, and destroyed.

And it was time to make them pay.

Silas powered down his terminal, the hum of the holographic display fading into silence. The shadows of doubt still lingered, but they no longer held him captive. He didn't need to trust his memories to trust himself.

As he stepped out into the rain-soaked streets, his pulse scanner tucked safely in his coat, Silas Kane knew one thing for certain: the fight wasn't over.

It was just beginning.

Chapter 13: The Key Memory

Silas Kane sat alone in the sterile silence of his apartment, the world outside reduced to the faint hum of traffic and the occasional patter of rain. The black device lay on his desk, its surface smooth and unyielding, hiding the answers he had fought so hard to uncover. It had taken countless close calls, painful revelations, and moments of near-despair, but he was finally here.

This was the moment he would dive into the key memory—the one that held the answers to everything.

His pulse quickened as he adjusted the neural interface on his temples. The weight of the device pressed heavily against his skin, a reminder of the countless dives that had brought him to this point. Each retrieval had taken a piece of him, blurring the lines between his past and the fragments of others' memories. But this time was different. This time, the memory wasn't just a clue. It was the truth.

And it was his.

The neural dive began with a sharp jolt, the real world dissolving into a cascade of light and sound. Silas braced himself as the fragmented edges of the memory formed around him, their jagged pieces fitting together like a shattered mirror reassembling itself. The sensation was disorienting, a swirl of emotions and images pulling him in every direction at once.

He landed in a room he didn't recognize but instinctively knew was significant. The walls were lined with monitors displaying neural scans, their screens pulsing with waves of electric blue. The air was cold and sterile, the faint hum of machinery filling the silence.

In the center of the room stood a chair—sleek, metallic, and ominously familiar. Silas's heart clenched as he realized it was the same chair from his fragmented memories, the one he had been strapped to during the experiments. And sitting in the chair was a younger version of himself.

The younger Silas was restrained, his wrists and ankles bound by sleek cuffs that glowed faintly with a pulsing red light. His face was pale, his eyes wide with a mixture of fear and defiance. A man in a lab coat stood before him, his face sharp and angular, his piercing blue eyes filled with cold calculation.

"Subject 21 is ready," the man said, his voice devoid of emotion. "Proceed with the synchronization test."

Another figure entered the room—a woman with a commanding presence, her dark suit tailored perfectly to her form. Silas recognized her immediately. She was one of the enforcers he had encountered during his investigation, a high-ranking operative of Aegis.

"Are you sure he can handle it?" the woman asked, her tone skeptical.

The man in the lab coat nodded. "His neural architecture is stable, and his memory retention exceeds projected parameters. If this works, he'll be the key to unlocking the full potential of Project Umbra."

"And if it doesn't?" the woman pressed, her gaze sharp.

"Then we'll start over with Subject 22," the man replied, his tone cold and matter-of-fact.

The woman's lips curled into a faint smirk. "Let's hope it doesn't come to that."

The memory shifted, pulling Silas deeper into the scene. He could feel the younger version of himself struggling against the restraints, his panic growing as the helmet-like device was lowered onto his head. The room filled with a low hum as the synchronization process began, the monitors displaying rapid spikes in neural activity.

Silas could feel the pain as if it were happening to him in real time—a sharp, blinding sensation that tore through his mind like a storm. He screamed, the sound echoing through the room, but the figures around him didn't react. They were too focused on the data streaming across the monitors.

"Neural synchronization at 85%," the man in the lab coat reported, his tone clinical. "Increasing memory implantation frequency."

The younger Silas's screams grew louder as the pain intensified. Fragments of memories—false and real—flooded his mind, their edges blurring together in a chaotic swirl. Faces he didn't recognize, places he had never been, and moments that weren't his all clashed for dominance, creating a fractured mosaic of a life he didn't fully understand.

And then, amidst the chaos, a single memory emerged, sharp and clear.

Silas was no longer in the lab. He was standing in a small, dimly lit room, the air heavy with the scent of antiseptic and fear. A man lay on a cot in the corner, his face pale and gaunt. It was Dr. Marcus Kane—his father.

"Silas," his father said, his voice weak but steady. "You have to stop them."

Silas felt his throat tighten as he stepped closer. "Dad, I don't understand. What's happening?"

"They've been using us," his father said, his eyes filled with sorrow. "Aegis doesn't care about the truth. They only care about control. Project Umbra—it's not about helping people. It's about owning them."

Silas shook his head, the weight of his father's words pressing down on him. "But why me? Why us?"

His father reached out, his hand trembling as it rested on Silas's arm. "Because we were expendable. They took our memories, our lives, and turned them into tools for their agenda. But it's not too late. You can stop them."

"How?" Silas asked, his voice breaking.

His father's grip tightened, his gaze fierce despite his frailty. "Find the core memory—the one they tried to erase. It's the key to everything."

The scene shifted again, pulling Silas back into the lab. The younger version of himself was unconscious now, the synchronization process complete. The man in the lab coat removed the helmet, his expression one of satisfaction.

"It's done," he said, turning to the woman in the suit. "Subject 21 is ready."

"And the memory?" the woman asked.

"Locked away," the man replied. "He won't remember it unless the failsafe is triggered."

"Good," the woman said, her tone cold. "Let's hope it stays that way."

Silas gasped as he was pulled out of the memory, his neural interface disconnecting with a sharp jolt. He ripped the device off his temples, his chest heaving as he tried to process what he had seen.

The key memory—the one his father had spoken of—was still buried deep within his mind, locked away by Aegis's manipulations. But he knew it existed, and he knew it was the answer to everything.

For the next several hours, Silas worked tirelessly to decrypt the remaining files from the black device. He cross-referenced the data with the fragments of his memories, searching for any clue that could lead him to the core memory. The process was painstaking, each breakthrough coming with its own set of questions.

Finally, he found it—a set of coordinates buried deep within the metadata of the files. They pointed to a location outside the city, a secluded facility hidden in the mountains.

Silas knew what he had to do. The key memory was there, waiting to be uncovered. And this time, he wouldn't stop until he had the truth.

As Silas prepared for the journey ahead, he couldn't shake the weight of what he had discovered. Aegis had taken everything from him—his past, his family, his identity. But they hadn't taken his will to fight.

The answers were within reach, and Silas Kane was ready to face whatever lay ahead.

Chapter 14: The Betrayal

The train hummed quietly as it sped through the outskirts of the city, the rhythmic clatter of steel on steel a constant backdrop to Silas Kane's turbulent thoughts. The coordinates he'd uncovered from the decrypted files pointed to a remote facility hidden in the mountains, far from prying eyes. It was the last piece of the puzzle, the place where the truth about Project Umbra—and his stolen memories—waited to be uncovered.

Yet the journey felt heavier than the destination. Silas leaned against the cool glass of the window, his reflection fractured by streaks of rain. The adrenaline that had propelled him through near-death encounters and revelations of his manipulated past had worn thin, leaving only exhaustion and doubt.

But most of all, it was the question of trust that gnawed at him.

The question had arisen subtly at first, planted like a seed during his last encounter with Nadine Cross's files. Among the fragments was a communication log—a series of encrypted messages between high-ranking Aegis operatives. At first, the exchanges were clinical, focused on logistics and data. But as Silas dug deeper, one message stood out:

"Ensure Subject 21 remains under control. Leverage internal assets as needed."

The term *"internal assets"* had been vague, but it implied betrayal. Someone close to Silas was complicit, feeding information back to Aegis. The thought chilled him to the core, especially as he mentally cataloged the few people he had trusted with his mission.

The shortlist was painfully short: Vera.

Vera had been his constant ally, the voice in his ear during high-stakes dives, the one person he believed he could count on when everything else fell apart. She had been the only anchor in his storm of fragmented memories and shifting truths.

But that trust now felt fragile.

Silas had confronted the thought again and again, searching for any sign—any anomaly in her behavior—that could confirm or dispel his suspicion. Her concern for his safety, her insistence on monitoring his vitals during dives, her occasional bouts of doubt about his methods—were these genuine acts of care, or calculated moves to keep him within Aegis's reach?

The train slowed as it approached a rural station, its brakes hissing like a warning. Silas gathered his things, the weight of the black device in his bag a constant reminder of the stakes. As he stepped onto the platform, the cold mountain air hit him like a slap, sharp and bracing. He pulled his coat tighter, scanning the horizon for the path that would lead him to the coordinates.

His comm system buzzed in his ear, and Vera's voice crackled through. "You there yet?"

Silas hesitated, his grip tightening on the strap of his bag. "I just got off the train," he said, keeping his tone neutral.

"Good," Vera replied, her voice warm but edged with tension. "This place gives me the creeps. Be careful."

Silas nodded absently, though she couldn't see him. "I'll call when I'm inside."

"Silas," Vera added, her voice softer now. "You don't have to do this alone."

The words struck a nerve, the offer of help both comforting and suspicious. Silas forced a smile into his voice. "Thanks, Vera. I'll be fine."

He ended the call before she could respond, his chest tightening as he made his way toward the facility.

The facility was exactly as the coordinates had described: a nondescript building nestled deep within the forest, its gray walls blending seamlessly with the rocky landscape. It was the kind of place you'd only find if you knew where to look. Silas approached cautiously, his pulse scanner ready as he scanned for security measures.

The entrance was unassuming, a heavy metal door set into the side of the building. Silas bypassed the lock with practiced ease, his heart pounding as the door swung open to reveal a dimly lit corridor. The air inside was cold and sterile, the faint hum of machinery echoing through the space.

He moved quickly, his steps silent as he navigated the labyrinth of hallways. The building seemed abandoned, but Silas knew better. Aegis wouldn't leave a place like this unguarded.

He found the central lab after several minutes of searching. The room was vast, its walls lined with monitors and data terminals. In the center stood a chair identical to the one from his memories, its metallic surface gleaming under the fluorescent lights.

Silas approached cautiously, his eyes scanning the room for any signs of movement. As he reached the terminal, his pulse scanner buzzed faintly, detecting an active signal. Someone was nearby.

Before he could react, the door behind him slammed shut. Silas spun around, his pulse scanner raised, as a figure stepped out of the shadows.

"Vera?" he said, disbelief flooding his voice.

She stood there, her expression unreadable, a tablet in her hand. Her presence was both a relief and a betrayal, the conflicting emotions crashing over Silas like a wave.

"You shouldn't have come here," she said, her tone low and tense.

Silas's grip on the pulse scanner tightened. "You knew about this place," he said, his voice edged with anger. "You knew what Aegis was doing, and you didn't tell me."

Vera sighed, her shoulders slumping as she took a step closer. "It's not that simple, Silas."

"Then explain it to me," he snapped. "Because right now, it looks like you've been feeding them information. Like you've been working against me this entire time."

Vera flinched at his words, but her expression hardened. "I was trying to protect you."

"Protect me?" Silas echoed, his voice rising. "By lying to me? By letting them turn my life into a nightmare?"

Vera set the tablet on the terminal, her gaze meeting his. "You don't understand what you're dealing with, Silas. Aegis isn't just some corrupt corporation. They're a system. You can't beat them."

Silas shook his head, his chest tightening with a mix of anger and betrayal. "So you decided to join them?"

"I didn't have a choice!" Vera shouted, her voice breaking. "They threatened my family, Silas. They gave me an ultimatum: help them monitor you, or lose everything."

Her words hung in the air, heavy with regret. Silas felt his anger waver, replaced by a deep sense of betrayal. "You should have told me," he said quietly. "We could have fought them together."

Vera's eyes filled with tears as she shook her head. "You don't understand. They don't leave loose ends, Silas. You think you're close to the truth, but you don't know what you're up against."

Before Silas could respond, the room filled with the sound of approaching footsteps. Vera's expression shifted to one of panic as she grabbed the tablet and turned to him.

"They're coming," she said urgently. "You need to get out of here."

"I'm not leaving without answers," Silas replied, his voice firm.

Vera hesitated, her gaze flicking between him and the door. Finally, she pressed the tablet into his hands. "Take this. It has everything—the truth about Project Umbra, about Aegis, about you."

"What about you?" Silas asked, his voice softening.

Vera gave him a sad smile. "I made my choice a long time ago. This is yours now."

Before Silas could stop her, she turned and stepped into the hallway, her voice echoing through the lab. "He's in here!"

The footsteps grew louder as Silas stared at the tablet in his hands. He didn't have time to process the weight of her betrayal—or her sacrifice. With one last glance at the lab, he bolted toward the emergency exit, the tablet clutched tightly against his chest.

The forest was dark and unforgiving as Silas ran, the sounds of pursuit fading into the distance. His mind raced as he tried to make sense of everything. Vera's betrayal, her confession, the truth she had handed him—it all blurred together in a storm of emotions.

When he finally reached the safety of a secluded clearing, he collapsed against a tree, his breath coming in ragged gasps. He powered on the tablet, its screen lighting up with files and reports that promised answers—but at a cost.

As the truth unfolded before him, Silas realized two things: Vera's betrayal had been born of desperation, and the battle he was fighting was far bigger than he had ever imagined.

Chapter 15: The Memory Vault

The tablet's screen illuminated Silas Kane's face as he scrolled through file after file, each revelation cutting deeper than the last. The clearing he'd stopped in was silent, save for the faint rustle of wind through the trees and the distant hum of the facility he'd just escaped. The world felt both eerily quiet and impossibly vast, a sharp contrast to the storm raging in Silas's mind.

The files Vera had handed him painted a picture far worse than he had anticipated. Project Umbra wasn't just an experiment in memory extraction—it was a blueprint for control, a system designed to reshape reality by rewriting the collective consciousness. And it wasn't just theoretical. The Memory Vault, a central database of extracted memories and manipulated identities, had already been operational for years.

The coordinates for the Vault were buried in the metadata of the files. Silas stared at them, the weight of the decision before him pressing down like a physical force. If he went to the Vault, he'd uncover the full extent of Aegis's operations. But it also meant walking directly into the lion's den.

For a moment, doubt flickered in his mind. Was he prepared for what he might find? Could he face the truth and survive it?

He took a deep breath, steeling himself. *You've come this far. There's no turning back now.*

The Vault's location was deep in the mountains, hidden beneath a disused mining facility. Silas approached cautiously, the jagged peaks towering above him like silent sentinels. The entrance was well-guarded, with drones patrolling the perimeter and guards stationed at key points. Aegis had spared no expense in protecting their secrets.

Silas crouched behind a boulder, studying the patterns of the patrols. His pulse scanner buzzed faintly in his pocket, a comforting reminder of the tools at his disposal. But even with his skills, breaching the Vault wouldn't be easy.

"Alright," he muttered to himself. "Let's see what you're hiding."

He waited until one of the drones passed overhead, its sensors sweeping the area before moving on. Then, with practiced precision, he darted across the open ground, keeping low and out of sight. The entrance to the facility loomed ahead—a heavy steel door embedded in the mountainside, flanked by two guards.

Silas reached for the neural disruptor he'd salvaged from Vera's files, a small but powerful device capable of scrambling short-range communications. He activated it, the faint hum of its activation filling the air.

The guards stiffened as their earpieces crackled, their connection to the central network severed. Silas moved quickly, taking them down with two well-placed bursts from his pulse scanner. The guards crumpled to the ground, unconscious but alive.

Silas bypassed the door's security system, the lock disengaging with a soft click. He slipped inside, the darkness of the tunnel swallowing him whole.

The interior of the facility was a stark contrast to the rugged exterior. Sleek, metallic walls lined the corridors, their surfaces glowing faintly with embedded lights. The air was cold and sterile, the faint hum of machinery echoing through the space.

Silas navigated the labyrinthine halls, relying on the map Vera had included in the tablet's files. The Vault was located at the heart of the facility, its entrance guarded by a biometric security system. Silas's pulse scanner buzzed as he approached, detecting the layers of defenses in place.

"Of course," he muttered, eyeing the complex system. Aegis hadn't made it easy, but Silas wasn't one to back down from a challenge.

He pulled out a modified neural key, a device he'd designed during his years as a memory retriever. It bypassed standard biometric locks by mimicking the neural patterns of authorized personnel. Silas connected it to the system, holding his breath as the device worked its magic.

After a tense moment, the lock disengaged, and the Vault's doors slid open with a soft hiss.

The room beyond was massive, a cavernous space filled with rows upon rows of servers. The air was thick with the hum of machinery, the lights from the servers casting an eerie glow. At the center of the room stood a massive console, its screens displaying a web of interconnected data points.

Silas approached the console, his pulse quickening as he activated the interface. The screen came to life, revealing a sprawling database labeled **"Memory Vault – Core Operations."**

"Let's see what you're hiding," Silas said, his fingers flying across the keyboard.

The files within the Vault were staggering in scope. Every memory extracted by Aegis, every manipulation performed as part of Project Umbra, was cataloged and stored here. Silas scrolled through the records, his chest tightening as he recognized names and faces.

Eleanor Laramie. Nadine Cross. Dr. Marcus Kane. Each entry contained detailed logs of their memories, their lives reduced to data points in Aegis's vast network.

But it wasn't just individuals. Entire communities had been targeted, their collective memories rewritten to suit Aegis's agenda. Silas's stomach churned as he read reports of fabricated histories, false events implanted to manipulate public perception.

"They're not just controlling people," he muttered. "They're rewriting reality."

Silas searched the database for his own records, his hands trembling as he accessed the files. The entries confirmed what he had long suspected: his memories had been altered repeatedly, key events erased or replaced to shape him into the perfect subject for Project Umbra.

One file stood out, marked **"Subject 21 – Core Memory Archive."** Silas opened it, his breath catching as a series of images and videos unfolded before him. They were fragments of his life, both familiar and foreign, each one a piece of the puzzle he had been trying to solve.

But one memory was locked, its data encrypted with the highest level of security. Silas's heart raced as he worked to bypass the encryption, his determination fueled by the knowledge that this memory was the key to everything.

The memory unfolded slowly, its edges sharp and vivid. Silas was back in the lab, the metallic walls gleaming under the harsh fluorescent lights. He was strapped to the chair, the helmet-like device clamped onto his head.

The man in the lab coat stood before him, his face filled with a mixture of determination and regret. "You'll thank us one day, Silas," he said, his voice low. "We're giving you a gift."

Silas struggled against the restraints, his voice muffled by the pain coursing through his head. "You're taking everything from me!"

The man hesitated, his gaze flickering with doubt. "No," he said softly. "We're making you into something greater."

The memory fractured, shifting to a new scene. Silas was in a small, dimly lit room, his father lying on a cot in the corner. Dr. Marcus Kane's voice was weak but filled with urgency as he spoke.

"They think they've erased it," his father said, his eyes locking onto Silas. "But the truth is still in you. Find the Vault, Silas. Find the truth."

The memory ended abruptly, leaving Silas staring at the console. His father had known about the Vault, had known that Aegis's manipulations weren't infallible. The truth was buried deep within the data, waiting to be uncovered.

Silas accessed the final file in the archive, a blueprint labeled **"Umbra – Worldstream Integration."** The document detailed Aegis's ultimate plan: to connect the Vault to a global network, allowing them to rewrite memories on a massive scale. Governments, corporations, entire populations—no one would be immune.

"They're not just rewriting reality," Silas whispered. "They're erasing free will."

Before he could process the full implications, the sound of footsteps echoed through the Vault. Silas turned, his pulse scanner ready, as a group of Aegis operatives entered the room.

"You've seen too much," their leader said, his tone cold and final.

Silas gritted his teeth, his determination hardening into resolve. "You can't stop the truth," he said, his voice steady.

The operatives advanced, but Silas was ready. He fired the pulse scanner, the room erupting into chaos as he fought to protect the data. Every move, every decision, was fueled by the knowledge that this was bigger than him. The truth had to survive, no matter the cost.

As the dust settled, Silas stood amidst the wreckage, the tablet clutched tightly in his hand. The Memory Vault was compromised, but the data he had extracted was safe. He had what he needed to expose Aegis, to dismantle their plans and reclaim the truth.

But the battle was far from over.

The mountain air was crisp as Silas emerged from the facility, his body battered but his spirit unbroken. He looked out at the horizon, the first rays of dawn breaking through the darkness.

The truth was finally within reach, and Silas Kane wasn't going to stop until the world knew it.

Chapter 16: Truth and Consequences

The streets of the city felt different now. The usual hum of life—cars rushing by, the chatter of pedestrians, the blinking neon signs—seemed muted, distant. Silas Kane walked among the crowds unnoticed, the weight of the tablet in his bag pulling at his shoulder like an anchor. Every step carried him closer to a decision he couldn't take back, a choice that would ripple far beyond his own life.

He had spent days decrypting the data extracted from the Memory Vault, piecing together the full scope of Aegis's operation. Project Umbra was more than a conspiracy—it was a global framework for manipulation, a system capable of rewriting not just individual memories but entire narratives. History itself was at risk of becoming a tool for control.

And now, Silas was the only one who could stop it.

But at what cost?

He slipped into his apartment, locking the door behind him. The air inside was stale, the blinds drawn to block out the outside world. His terminal sat on the desk, its screen dark, waiting for him to make his move. Silas placed the tablet beside it, his hands trembling as he powered it on.

The files appeared on the screen, their stark text and images a damning testament to Aegis's reach. Names of politicians, CEOs, journalists—all puppets whose memories had been manipulated to serve the company's agenda. Entire communities had been targeted, their collective histories rewritten to eliminate dissent and ensure compliance.

Silas stared at the screen, his mind racing. If he released this information, it would expose Aegis for what they truly were. But it would also make him a target, not just for the company but for every powerful entity that had benefited from their manipulations. The truth wouldn't just bring justice—it would bring chaos.

The comm system buzzed, pulling Silas from his thoughts. He hesitated before answering, Vera's voice crackling through the static.

"Silas," she said, her tone heavy with exhaustion. "I'm glad you're still alive."

"Barely," he replied, his voice strained. "You?"

"I'm holding on," Vera said. "But you've got to move fast. Aegis knows you have the Vault's data. They're already mobilizing."

Silas rubbed his temples, the weight of the decision pressing down on him. "If I release this, it'll bring them down," he said. "But it'll also destroy lives. People will lose everything—their jobs, their families, their sense of reality. Is it worth it?"

Vera was silent for a moment before replying. "That's not a question I can answer for you, Silas. But I can tell you this: the world deserves to know the truth, no matter how painful it is."

Her words hung in the air, a stark reminder of the responsibility that now rested on Silas's shoulders. He thanked her and ended the call, his focus returning to the terminal.

Silas opened the first file, a detailed report on the synchronization process used in Project Umbra. The document described how memories were extracted, altered, and implanted, with chilling precision. Each step was outlined in cold, clinical terms, reducing human lives to mere data points.

The next file was even worse. It contained logs of experiments performed on unwilling subjects, many of whom had been declared missing or dead. Their memories had been stripped away, their identities erased and rewritten to serve Aegis's goals.

One entry made Silas pause. It was a log detailing his own involvement in Project Umbra, marked **"Subject 21 – Full Report."** He hesitated before opening it, unsure if he was ready to confront the full truth about his past.

But he knew he couldn't stop now.

The report was brutally thorough, outlining every experiment performed on Silas during his time as a subject. It detailed how his memories had been manipulated to create a false narrative, one that would make him more susceptible to Aegis's influence.

But it also revealed something unexpected: a hidden failsafe implanted in his neural architecture. If triggered, it would erase all traces of his involvement in Project Umbra, leaving him with no memory of the truth he had uncovered.

"They built me to be expendable," Silas muttered, his voice thick with anger.

The knowledge filled him with a renewed sense of purpose. Aegis had tried to control him, to turn him into a tool for their agenda. But they had failed. And now, he had the power to dismantle their empire.

Silas leaned back in his chair, the decision looming over him like a storm cloud. If he released the files, it would expose Aegis's crimes and potentially bring their operations to a halt. But it would also paint a target on his back, leaving him vulnerable to retaliation.

He thought of Eleanor Laramie, Nadine Cross, his father—people who had paid the ultimate price for standing against Aegis. Their sacrifices weighed heavily on his mind, a reminder that the truth often came at a cost.

He also thought of Vera, who had betrayed him out of desperation but had ultimately helped him uncover the truth. Her actions had been flawed, but they had been driven by a desire to protect what mattered most to her. Could Silas make the same claim?

As the hours ticked by, Silas worked tirelessly to prepare the files for release. He created backups, encrypted the data, and set up a network of secure servers to ensure the information would reach the right people. Journalists, whistleblower organizations, activists—he compiled a list of recipients who would know what to do with the truth.

But even as he worked, doubt lingered in the back of his mind. Was he doing the right thing? Would the world be better off knowing the full extent of Aegis's crimes, or would the truth only lead to more suffering?

The comm system buzzed again, startling him. This time, it was an unknown number. Silas hesitated before answering, his heart pounding as a deep, unfamiliar voice filled the room.

"You've made a lot of noise, Kane," the voice said. "And you've made some powerful enemies."

"Who is this?" Silas demanded, his pulse quickening.

"A friend," the voice replied. "Or at least, someone who sees value in what you're trying to do. But let me give you a piece of advice: releasing that data will change everything, and not necessarily for the better."

Silas frowned, his grip tightening on the edge of the desk. "You're saying I should just let Aegis get away with it?"

"No," the voice said. "But think carefully about the consequences. Once this truth is out, there's no putting it back. People will lose faith in the systems that govern their lives. Chaos will follow."

"Maybe chaos is what we need," Silas shot back.

"Maybe," the voice conceded. "But are you ready to live with that on your conscience?"

The call ended abruptly, leaving Silas alone with his thoughts.

When the files were finally ready, Silas sat back and stared at the terminal. His finger hovered over the send button, his mind racing with the possibilities. The decision felt impossibly heavy, the weight of the world resting on his shoulders.

He thought of the people whose lives had been destroyed by Aegis, the countless individuals whose memories had been stolen and rewritten. They deserved justice, and the world deserved to know the truth.

But he also thought of the chaos that would follow, the lives that would be upended by the revelations. Could he live with the consequences of his actions?

In the end, Silas made his choice.

The files went out in a burst of encrypted transmissions, spreading across the globe like wildfire. Within minutes, journalists and whistleblowers were receiving the data, their screens lighting up with the damning evidence of Aegis's crimes.

Silas sat back, his heart pounding as the enormity of what he had done sank in. The truth was out, and there was no going back.

As the first reports began to appear online, Silas felt a mix of relief and fear. He had done what he believed was right, but he knew the battle was far from over. Aegis wouldn't go down without a fight, and he would have to stay one step ahead if he wanted to survive.

But for the first time in a long time, Silas felt a glimmer of hope. The truth was out, and the world was watching.

Chapter 17: The Final Extraction

The sterile hum of fluorescent lights greeted Silas Kane as he stepped into the vast, cavernous chamber that lay at the heart of Aegis's final stronghold. The walls were lined with rows of servers humming softly, each one a repository of countless stolen lives. At the far end of the chamber stood a sleek metallic chair—the focal point of every nightmare that had plagued Silas since he first discovered the truth.

The **Memory Extraction Core.**

This was where it had all begun. And this was where it would end.

The data he'd released to the world had ignited a firestorm. Whistleblowers, journalists, and activists were now picking apart the intricate web of lies that Aegis had spun. But the company wasn't beaten yet. Their vast resources and hidden influence had allowed them to regroup and counterattack. Silas had been hunted relentlessly since the files went public, forcing him to navigate a world even more dangerous than the one he thought he knew.

And now, after weeks of evasion, his journey had brought him here: the epicenter of Aegis's power and the place that held the last piece of the puzzle.

The memory he had avoided for so long.

The chamber's silence was broken by the sound of slow, deliberate footsteps. Silas turned to see a figure approaching—a tall man in a tailored black suit, his silver hair slicked back, and his piercing blue eyes filled with cold calculation.

"Silas Kane," the man said, his voice smooth and controlled. "You've caused quite a mess."

Silas raised his pulse scanner, the device humming softly in his hand. "It's over," he said, his voice steady despite the storm raging inside him. "The truth is out. People know what you've done."

The man smiled faintly, his expression one of faint amusement. "The truth? You think what you've revealed is the truth? That's just the tip of the iceberg. You don't understand the scope of what we're doing here."

"I understand enough," Silas shot back. "You've stolen lives, rewritten memories, and twisted reality to suit your agenda. And now, you're going to pay for it."

The man's smile faded, replaced by a look of cold determination. "You're bold, I'll give you that. But you're also naïve. Do you really think you can stop us? Aegis isn't just a company—it's an idea. And ideas are much harder to kill."

The man gestured toward the Memory Extraction Core, its metallic surface gleaming under the harsh lights. "But since you're so eager to understand, let me show you what you've been avoiding."

Silas hesitated, his grip on the pulse scanner tightening. "What are you talking about?"

The man's gaze sharpened, his voice dropping to a low, menacing tone. "You've been running from the truth, Silas. The memory you've buried, the one you refuse to face—it's the key to everything."

Silas felt a chill run down his spine. He had spent years trying to uncover the truth about Aegis, but there was one memory he had never been able to retrieve, one fragment of his past that remained locked away.

And now, he realized, the man was right. He couldn't win this fight without confronting it.

Reluctantly, Silas approached the Core, his heart pounding as he sat in the chair. The metallic restraints clicked into place, holding him firmly but not uncomfortably. The man stepped behind the console, his fingers flying across the holographic interface.

"This memory," the man said, his tone almost clinical, "is the first one we took from you. The foundation of everything that followed."

Silas clenched his fists, bracing himself as the device powered on. A sharp jolt shot through his mind, and the world around him dissolved into a cascade of light and sound.

The memory unfolded slowly, its edges blurred like an old photograph. Silas found himself in a small, dimly lit room. A younger version of himself stood in the corner, his face pale and his eyes wide with fear.

Across the room, two figures argued heatedly. One was his father, Dr. Marcus Kane, his voice filled with anger and desperation. The other was the man in the suit, his demeanor calm but menacing.

"You can't do this," Marcus said, his voice shaking. "He's just a child."

The man in the suit shook his head. "He's not just a child, Marcus. He's the future. With his neural architecture, we can perfect the synchronization process. He'll be the keystone of Project Umbra."

"No," Marcus said firmly, stepping between the man and Silas. "I won't let you turn him into a tool for your experiments."

The man's expression hardened. "You don't have a choice."

The memory fractured, shifting to a new scene. Silas was now strapped to the chair, the same one he was currently sitting in. His father stood beside him, his hands trembling as he adjusted the controls on the console.

"I'm sorry, Silas," Marcus said, his voice thick with emotion. "I couldn't stop them. But I'll make sure you don't lose yourself."

Silas felt a sharp pain in his head as the synchronization process began. Memories flooded his mind—real and fabricated—until he couldn't tell the difference. His screams echoed through the room, but his father's voice cut through the chaos.

"Remember this, Silas," Marcus said urgently. "They can take your memories, but they can't take who you are. Fight them. Find the truth."

The memory dissolved, pulling Silas back to the present. He gasped as the restraints released, his body trembling from the intensity of the experience. The man in the suit watched him closely, his expression unreadable.

"Now you understand," the man said softly. "You were never just a subject, Silas. You were the foundation of everything we've built."

Silas glared at him, his anger boiling over. "You destroyed my life. You took everything from me."

"And yet, here you are," the man replied, a faint smile tugging at his lips. "Stronger than anyone else we've ever tested. You're living proof that our work is necessary."

Silas stood, his pulse scanner raised. "Your work ends here."

The fight was brutal and chaotic, the room erupting into a cacophony of sound and light. Silas moved with a combination of precision and desperation, his every move driven by the memory of his father's sacrifice.

The man in the suit was a formidable opponent, his movements swift and calculated. But Silas's determination gave him an edge, his strikes landing with a force born of years of pain and anger.

Finally, with one last burst from his pulse scanner, Silas brought the man to his knees. The room fell silent, save for the hum of the machinery and Silas's ragged breathing.

Silas approached the console, his hands trembling as he accessed the Core's database. The files within were a treasure trove of evidence, detailing every experiment, every manipulation, every life Aegis had destroyed.

He inserted a data drive, copying the files as quickly as possible. The man in the suit watched him, his expression one of resignation.

"You think this will change anything?" the man asked. "The world isn't ready for the truth."

Silas didn't respond. He ejected the drive, slipping it into his pocket before turning to face the man.

"The world deserves the truth," he said. "And I'm going to make sure they get it."

As Silas walked away from the Core, the weight of his father's words echoed in his mind: *"They can take your memories, but they can't take who you are."*

He had reclaimed the truth, not just for himself, but for everyone Aegis had tried to silence. The fight wasn't over, but for the first time, Silas felt like he had the power to win.

Chapter 18: The Hunter Becomes the Hunted

The city was alive with whispers, the truth about Aegis spreading like wildfire. Leaks to journalists, viral exposés, and whistleblower accounts had painted a damning picture of a corporation whose reach extended into the highest levels of government, media, and law enforcement. Silas Kane had lit the match that started the fire, but now he was feeling the heat.

The data he'd extracted from the Memory Vault had revealed far more than he had anticipated. It wasn't just about the stolen lives or the manipulated memories—it was about him. Silas wasn't merely an investigator unraveling a conspiracy. He was the lynchpin of the entire operation.

And now, the hunters had become the hunted.

Silas sat in a rundown motel on the outskirts of the city, his pulse scanner on the table beside a stack of printed documents. The room was dark, save for the glow of his terminal as it displayed a holographic web of connections—names, places, and events all tied to Project Umbra.

At the center of the web was his own name: **Silas Kane – Subject 21.**

The files Vera had handed him had hinted at the truth, but it wasn't until he'd accessed the Vault that he understood the full scope of his role. Aegis hadn't just manipulated his memories—they had built him. Every choice he thought he'd made, every lead he thought he'd uncovered, had been orchestrated.

He wasn't just solving the case. He was the case.

The revelation had come with a single file buried deep in the Memory Vault: **"Phase Five – Subject 21 Activation Protocol."**

The document detailed how Silas had been groomed to play the role of an investigator, his false memories designed to give him the perfect combination of skills and motivation to uncover "the truth." But the truth he'd been chasing wasn't the real truth—it was a carefully constructed narrative designed to lead him exactly where Aegis wanted.

They had used him to expose their enemies, dismantle rival factions, and eliminate rogue operatives who had gone too far. Every victory he thought he'd won had been part of their plan.

A sharp knock at the door snapped Silas out of his thoughts. He grabbed the pulse scanner, his heart racing as he approached the door. He peered through the peephole, his stomach sinking when he saw the familiar figure on the other side.

"Vera," he muttered, his grip on the scanner tightening.

He opened the door cautiously, keeping the scanner at his side. Vera stepped inside, her expression a mix of relief and worry. She looked tired, her clothes disheveled and her eyes shadowed with exhaustion.

"We need to talk," she said, her voice low.

Silas closed the door, his jaw tightening. "Talk about what? How you've been working with Aegis this whole time? Or how you lied to me while they turned me into their puppet?"

Vera flinched but didn't back down. "I didn't know," she said, her voice steady despite the tension between them. "Not at first. I thought I was helping you. It wasn't until I saw the files from the Vault that I realized the truth."

Silas crossed his arms, his expression hard. "And now what? You expect me to trust you?"

"No," Vera admitted. "I expect you to hear me out. Because if we don't work together, they're going to win."

Reluctantly, Silas gestured for her to sit. Vera pulled out a small device and placed it on the table. It emitted a faint hum, a signal jammer designed to block any attempts to track their location.

"They're not just after you," Vera said, her tone serious. "They're after everyone who knows about Project Umbra. The leaks you released? They were a distraction. Aegis doesn't care about the fallout—they're already working on a new system, one that makes Umbra look like a prototype."

Silas frowned, his mind racing. "What are you talking about?"

Vera activated her terminal, pulling up a series of files labeled **"Worldstream Protocol."** The documents detailed a global network designed to integrate memory manipulation technology on an unprecedented scale. Unlike Umbra, which relied on isolated operations, Worldstream would link entire populations to a centralized system, allowing Aegis to rewrite reality in real time.

"This is their endgame," Vera said, her voice grim. "And they're using you to get there."

The pieces began to fall into place, each one more horrifying than the last. Silas realized that the information he had leaked wasn't just about exposing Aegis—it was about consolidating their power. By dismantling their rivals and rogue elements, he had unknowingly cleared the path for Worldstream.

He slammed his fist on the table, the force rattling the scanner. "They played me," he said through gritted teeth. "Every step of the way."

Vera placed a hand on his arm, her touch hesitant but firm. "That's why we have to stop them. Together."

Silas looked at her, the weight of his anger and betrayal colliding with the faint glimmer of hope she offered. He didn't trust her—not completely—but he knew he couldn't do this alone.

"What's the plan?" he asked, his voice laced with determination.

The first step was to track down the core of Worldstream. Vera had uncovered a lead—a hidden facility located deep beneath the city, accessible only through a series of encrypted pathways. The facility housed the central server that controlled the network, as well as the team responsible for implementing the final phase.

Breaking into the facility would be nearly impossible, but Silas was no stranger to impossible tasks. With Vera's help, he mapped out a plan, each step carefully calculated to avoid detection.

But even as they worked, Silas couldn't shake the feeling that they were already being watched.

The infiltration began at midnight, the city shrouded in darkness. Silas and Vera moved through the underground tunnels, their footsteps echoing softly against the damp walls. The air was thick with the smell of rust and decay, a stark reminder of how far they had fallen from the glittering world above.

The entrance to the facility was hidden behind a series of false walls and biometric locks. Silas used his neural key to bypass the security systems, his hands steady despite the tension in the air.

As they entered the main chamber, the scale of the operation became clear. Rows of servers stretched as far as the eye could see, their lights blinking rhythmically like a digital heartbeat. At the center of the room was a massive console, its screens displaying a live feed of the Worldstream network.

"This is it," Vera said, her voice barely above a whisper.

Silas nodded, his focus narrowing. "Let's shut it down."

The console's interface was a labyrinth of code and encryption, each layer designed to protect the system from intrusion. Silas worked quickly, his fingers flying across the keyboard as he bypassed the safeguards one by one.

But just as he reached the final layer, an alarm blared, the sound cutting through the air like a knife. Vera's eyes widened as the doors slammed shut, trapping them inside.

"They know we're here," she said, her voice filled with urgency.

Silas didn't respond. He focused on the console, his mind racing as he tried to finish the override. The room filled with the sound of approaching footsteps, the clatter of boots echoing off the walls.

The first wave of enforcers burst into the room, their weapons drawn. Silas grabbed his pulse scanner, firing off bursts of energy as he protected the console. Vera moved beside him, her own weapon humming as she took down the attackers with precision.

The fight was chaotic, the air thick with smoke and the hum of energy weapons. Silas's focus was split between the battle and the console, each second bringing them closer to either victory or defeat.

Finally, with one last keystroke, the system shut down. The lights on the servers dimmed, the hum of the machinery fading into silence.

"We did it," Vera said, her voice filled with relief.

But Silas's victory was short-lived. As the enforcers regrouped, he realized they had only just begun to fight.

The room erupted into chaos once more, Silas and Vera fighting side by side as they held their ground. Every move was a battle for survival, every second a test of their resolve.

As the dust settled, Silas stood amidst the wreckage, his body battered but unbroken. He looked at Vera, her expression one of determination and exhaustion.

The fight wasn't over, but for the first time, Silas felt like he was truly in control.

Chapter 19: Epilogue: The Memory Keeper

The city was quiet in the early morning light, its usual cacophony dulled to a faint hum as the world began to stir. Silas Kane stood on the rooftop of a weathered building overlooking the skyline, the wind tugging at his coat. His pulse scanner, now silent, hung loosely in his hand—a relic of battles fought and truths uncovered.

Below him, the world churned with the aftermath of Aegis's downfall. The files he'd leaked had ignited a firestorm, exposing decades of lies, manipulation, and stolen lives. Public outrage had erupted like a tidal wave, dismantling the corporation's grip on power. Protests filled the streets, investigations were launched, and high-ranking officials were being held accountable for their complicity.

But victory came with a price.

Silas's comm buzzed softly, pulling him from his thoughts. He tapped his earpiece, Vera's voice cutting through the static.

"They just announced another round of arrests," she said. "Three senators, two CEOs, and half a dozen law enforcement officials. Aegis is unraveling faster than anyone expected."

Silas exhaled, the weight of exhaustion heavy in his chest. "And the Worldstream servers?"

"Gone," Vera replied. "The facility you hit was the last of them. The network is offline for good."

Silas nodded, though the satisfaction he expected didn't come. "What about the people they manipulated? The memories they rewrote?"

Vera hesitated before answering. "That's... harder. Some of the damage is irreversible. The neural pathways they altered can't always be restored."

Silas closed his eyes, the guilt washing over him like a tidal wave. For all the lives he had saved, countless others remained broken, their identities fractured beyond repair.

"I'll call you later," he said, cutting the connection before Vera could respond.

The walk back to his apartment was slow, each step weighed down by the enormity of what he had done. The streets were lined with posters and graffiti, all bearing the same phrase: **"Truth Will Out."**

The people believed they had won, that the truth had set them free. But Silas knew better. The truth was messy, complicated. It didn't always heal—it often hurt, leaving scars that never fully faded.

When he reached his apartment, he hesitated at the door. The space inside felt foreign now, its walls a reminder of the man he had been before the world turned upside down. He stepped inside, the quiet enveloping him like a shroud.

The terminal on his desk blinked softly, its screen displaying the last of the files from the Memory Vault. Silas stared at them for a long moment before sitting down, his fingers hovering over the keyboard.

He opened one of the files, a record of the experiments performed on him during his time as Subject 21. The data was cold and clinical, each line a reminder of how Aegis had stolen his life, piece by piece.

But as he scrolled through the file, something caught his eye—a note buried deep within the metadata:

"Subject retains high neural adaptability. Potential candidate for Phase Six."

Silas frowned, his heart pounding as he searched for more information. The phrase "Phase Six" appeared only once in the database, attached to a single document labeled **"Confidential – Future Applications."**

He opened it, the words on the screen making his blood run cold.

The document detailed plans for a new iteration of memory manipulation technology, one designed to integrate seamlessly into everyday life. Unlike Project Umbra or Worldstream, this system wouldn't require invasive procedures or centralized networks. Instead, it would be embedded into wearable devices, smart systems, and everyday interfaces.

"Phase Six will not require direct control. Memory recalibration will occur organically, shaped by the user's environment and interactions. The technology will be invisible, its influence pervasive."

Silas's stomach churned as he realized the implications. Even with Aegis dismantled, their vision for the future had already taken root. The seeds of memory manipulation had been sown, and it was only a matter of time before someone else picked up where they had left off.

The weight of the revelation settled over Silas like a storm cloud. He had fought so hard to expose the truth, only to discover that the battle was far from over. The tools Aegis had created were too valuable, too tempting for the world to ignore.

The comm buzzed again, but this time Silas ignored it. He couldn't bear to hear Vera's voice, couldn't face the questions she would inevitably ask.

Instead, he opened a blank file on his terminal and began to write.

The document was titled **"The Memory Keeper's Manifesto."** It was a record of everything he had uncovered, from Aegis's early experiments to the dark future their technology promised. It was raw, unpolished, but it was honest—a blueprint for anyone willing to fight against the tide of manipulation.

Silas wrote for hours, his fingers flying across the keyboard as he poured his thoughts onto the page. He didn't stop until the sun began to rise, the first rays of light cutting through the darkness.

When he finished, he sat back and stared at the screen. The manifesto was both a confession and a warning, a plea for humanity to guard against the dangers of tampering with the mind.

Silas saved the document and uploaded it to a secure server, its contents encrypted and distributed across multiple nodes. If anything happened to him, the manifesto would be released automatically, ensuring that his story—and the truth—would survive.

He leaned back in his chair, the exhaustion finally catching up with him. The fight had taken everything from him, leaving scars he wasn't sure would ever heal. But for the first time in a long time, he felt a glimmer of peace.

The world wasn't perfect, and the battle was far from over. But Silas Kane had done his part. He had uncovered the truth, and he had shared it with the world.

What happened next was up to them.

As the morning light filled the room, Silas stood and walked to the window. He looked out at the city, its streets alive with the promise of a new day. Somewhere out there, the next chapter of the story was waiting to be written.

And for the first time, Silas was content to let it unfold without him.

Do Not Go Yet; One Last Thing To Do

If you enjoyed this book or found it useful, I'd be very grateful if you'd post a short review. Your support really does make a difference, and I read all the reviews personally so I can get your feedback and make this book even better.

. Support My Work

If you enjoyed this book and would like to see more like it, please consider making a donation. Your contributions will directly support the creation of future projects, enabling me to dedicate more time and resources to research, writing, and production.

How to Donate

BTC

bc1qs72228z6pauw3rk9tej9f6umu4y9gz289y3cvn

ETH

0xE1DAE6F656c900a4b24257b587ac0856E1e346D2

Thanks again for your support!

Don't miss out!

Visit the website below and you can sign up to receive emails whenever Timu Style publishes a new book. There's no charge and no obligation.

https://books2read.com/r/B-A-TGBUC-JCJIF

BOOKS 2 READ

Connecting independent readers to independent writers.

Did you love *The Memory Hunter: Hunted by Secrets, Haunted by Truth*? Then you should read *The Timekeeper's Journal: Secrets of the Past, Choices of the Present*[1] by Timu Style!

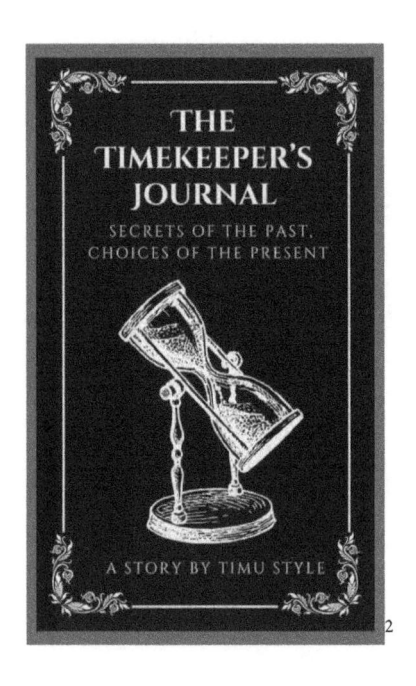

The Timekeeper's Journal: Secrets of the Past, Choices of the Present follows Dr. Eleanor Carter, a tenacious archaeologist on the verge of career failure, who stumbles upon an ancient journal that reveals secrets of long-lost civilizations and a time-altering artifact. As she deciphers the cryptic entries, Eleanor uncovers the power to momentarily reshape historical events. Yet each alteration ripples through her present, threatening those she holds dear. With rival scientist Dr. Simon

---

1. https://books2read.com/u/3nkGWK

2. https://books2read.com/u/3nkGWK

Blackwood desperate to control the artifact, Eleanor must navigate her loyalty to history against her personal attachments. This tale of adventure, ethical dilemmas, and mystery takes readers on a thrilling journey through time's fragile fabric, where every choice could rewrite destiny.

Also by Timu Style

Your Day, Your Way: Embracing Self-Love Over Birthday Wishes
The Timekeeper's Journal: Secrets of the Past, Choices of the Present
The Memory Hunter: Hunted by Secrets, Haunted by Truth

Milton Keynes UK
Ingram Content Group UK Ltd.
UKHW031047291124
451807UK00001B/49